# Caribbean Gold

## (Alicia Myles #3)

By

David Leadbeater

Copyright 2016 by David Leadbeater
ISBN: 978-1537788562

All rights reserved.
No part of this publication may be reproduced, distributed, or transmitted in any form or by any means, including photocopying, recording, or other electronic or mechanical methods, without the prior written permission of the publisher/author except in the case of brief quotations embodied in critical reviews and certain other non-commercial uses permitted by copyright law.
All characters in this book are fictitious, and any resemblance to actual persons living or dead is purely coincidental.

This ebook is for your personal enjoyment only. This ebook may not be re-sold or given away to other people. If you would like to share this ebook with another person, please purchase any additional copy for each reader. If you're reading this book and did not purchase it, or it was not purchased for your use only, then please return it and purchase your own copy. Thank you for respecting the hard work of this author.

Thriller, adventure, action, mystery, suspense, archaeological, military, historical

# Other Books by David Leadbeater:

### The Matt Drake Series
*The Bones of Odin (Matt Drake #1)*
*The Blood King Conspiracy (Matt Drake #2)*
*The Gates of hell (Matt Drake 3)*
*The Tomb of the Gods (Matt Drake #4)*
*Brothers in Arms (Matt Drake #5)*
*The Swords of Babylon (Matt Drake #6)*
*Blood Vengeance (Matt Drake #7)*
*Last Man Standing (Matt Drake #8)*
*The Plagues of Pandora (Matt Drake #9)*
*The Lost Kingdom (Matt Drake #10)*
*The Ghost Ships of Arizona (Matt Drake #11)*
*The Last Bazaar (Matt Drake #12)*
*The Edge of Armageddon (Matt Drake #13)*
*The Treasures of Saint Germain (Matt Drake #14)*

### The Alicia Myles Series
*Aztec Gold (Alicia Myles #1)*
*Crusader's Gold (Alicia Myles #2)*

### The Torsten Dahl Thriller Series
*Stand Your Ground (Dahl Thriller #1)*

**The Disavowed Series:**
*The Razor's Edge (Disavowed #1)*
*In Harm's Way (Disavowed #2)*
*Threat Level: Red (Disavowed #3)*

**The Chosen Few Series**
*Chosen (The Chosen Trilogy #1)*
*Guardians (The Chosen Tribology #2)*

**Short Stories**
*Walking with Ghosts (A short story)*
*A Whispering of Ghosts (A short story)*

Connect with the author on Twitter: @dleadbeater2011
Visit the author's website: **www.davidleadbeater.com**

All helpful, genuine comments are welcome. I would love to hear from you.
davidleadbeater2011@hotmail.co.uk

# Caribbean Gold

## CHAPTER ONE

Alicia Myles perched on the very edge of her economy plane seat, probably freaking out all those around her as the plane twitched in turbulence, but not really noticing or caring.

Her thoughts were far away, the light buffeting barely registering with her.

How quickly and randomly life spun. How fleeting its best moments. How quickly a bright future could turn into a vision from hell. It wasn't as though—this time at least—she'd made any mistakes. All her decisions had been made fairly, for good reasons. But still, she never seemed to be able to come out of any situation with a sense of peace.

In my life there has never been peace.

But dwelling now wasn't going to help her. She was a soldier, part of an elite team, but had taken a few days away to help out a friend. That friend—her old boss.

Michael Crouch had called at an incredibly poignant time. She remembered his words and her feelings like the sound of her own breath.

"I heard about Beau. I know what you guys are going through. I'm shattered that he betrayed the team and my trust. If you come to Jamaica now you can be part of our new venture, and I'll explain all I know."

*New venture* of course meant "latest treasure hunt". The Gold crew, as she thought of them, had little success since being a major part of the crusaders' gold quest a little while ago, coming up short at least twice. But then, not every hunt for ancient treasures was going to prove successful.

"Jamaica?" she had answered, mostly to give herself a little more thinking time.

"It's in the Caribbean."

"I *know* where it is, boss. Jeez."

Crouch had been her old boss when Alicia worked for a clandestine division of the British Special Forces.

"Nice climate. Great people. Rum. Scenery."

Alicia had shaken her head, still thinking. "Scenery? Really?"

"I'd really like you to come."

Alicia continued to run through her current situation. In a nutshell her old boyfriend had just betrayed everything she held dear, then died, and her new boyfriend was having trouble shrugging off the attentions of a certain irritating lifelong flame. A break, a brief getaway, was a very good idea.

"All right, boss. I'll come and brighten your days up. Tell Russo not to get too frisky and ask Healey how the quest for facial hair is going. Is Caitlyn still with you?"

"Yes. Hanging in there."

"Good. Then I'll see you in Jamaica."

"Kingston," Crouch said. "I'll text you the hotel details."

Alicia had been about to end the call, but a sliver of curiosity moved through her thoughts. "Why Jamaica?"

"Captain Morgan."

"Yeah, I was thinking of that for the plane ride. But why Jamaica?"

"Captain *Henry* Morgan. Oh it's a juicy one this is, Alicia. One of the most notorious and successful pirates in history, his treasure has never been found."

"Cool," Alicia said. "I'd rather look around for Jack Sparrow's alter ego if we're being honest."

"They named the rum after him."

*"What?"* Alicia was impressed. "Now that takes more than a modicum of infamy."

"Raider. Admiral. Privateer. Buccaneer. The star of many stories from a James Bond tale to *Pirates of the Caribbean*, John Steinbeck to Isaac Asimov. He amassed over two hundred thousand pieces of eight on one raid alone."

"Never found? I guess that's not unusual."

"We'll talk it through when you get here. Things might get a little nasty due to recent developments with Morgan, and some unsavory types are involved. You'll see."

"Mmmm. Nasty is what I do. What happened?"

"They found five of his ships."

*"Five?* Shit."

"And that's just the start of it. I'll see you in a few hours."

Alicia had dropped the cellphone into her pocket, made quick goodbyes and tried to ignore the hurt on her boyfriend's—Matt Drake's—eyes. She knew he'd imagined the worst, knowing her so well, but she'd made a heartfelt plea that this was essential and would help, and then skipped on out.

Well, not literally. Alicia didn't skip. She couldn't remember skipping or a stable home life. Only fighting. Her thoughts came around to the present day and she pictured herself sat rigid on the edge of the seat as the noisy plane zipped through the skies.

She glanced around. Men and women, kids and babies were either being excessively noisy or silently entertained, but that was all okay. She barely saw them. Just the soldier's quick assessment and then disinterest. A deeper problem haunted her. Something she hadn't mentioned even to Drake.

Beauregard Alain—Alicia's old boyfriend—had betrayed them all in the most terrible manner. He'd even tried to kill them before being taken down. If that wasn't bad enough, before he died he'd told Alicia to ask Crouch about why he'd betrayed them.

Ask Crouch.

The man she respected above all others. The man she'd

always been proud to call "boss". And Alicia Myles didn't take any fond nicknaming lightly. Quite the opposite in fact. The ones that usually made the grade were somewhat derogatory.

What's going on with you, Crouch?

Of course, it could be nothing. Just a way for a bad man to get further under her skin. She was certainly in the best position to challenge Crouch in her own inimitable way, but even she understood it needed to be done with tact.

The captain announced that they would soon be starting to descend, and the seatbelt sign was illuminated. Alicia stared over a woman's slight shoulder at the vista below and felt nothing of the excitement she knew she should. This job might end up being tinged with sadness.

She tried to concentrate on the facts Crouch had explained around Captain Morgan. If five of the guy's ships had been found then the security presence alone would be robust to say the least. All discoveries brought all kinds out of the woodwork—and she was thinking criminals. From the lowest, sniveling jackals hoping for a buck or two to the most complex conglomerate, searching for the money angle. But this...

This was one of the greatest pirates of the Spanish Main, the looter of looters that made the glistening Caribbean his own, personal world of dreams. Not only had he stolen, pillaged and destroyed but he'd had England's backing. Alicia imagined some might think it an odd state of affairs and steeped in the olden days, but had anything really changed? When you got right down to it weren't certain nations still out there pirating and helping themselves to the riches that belonged to others?

Days of the pirate long gone?

*Don't you believe it, honey,* Alicia smiled grimly to herself. She'd known a few Blackbeards in her time. And maybe even a Captain Flint. But Morgan? Who did she know that might be his equivalent now?

The plane fell sharply; the people around her grew further excited. And Alicia spent a few pleasant moments trying to pick a face from those she knew that might most fit the visage of a clever, successful buccaneer.

Trouble was—the best she could come up with was herself.

## CHAPTER TWO

Jamaica lay at the heart of the Caribbean, a dazzling, vibrant, multi-faceted jewel, its people a credit to its flamboyant reputation, its reputation earned throughout history. Alicia coped with the customs procedures as best she could and then walked out into the terminal, surrounded by what she thought of as a "safe turbulence", the grounded version of what they'd experienced in the air. People came from every side, wave after wave, buffeting and apologizing and continuing on their way. Alicia picked her way through and toward the bright light near the entrance, digging her sunglasses out of her hand luggage. At the same time, she fished out her cellphone and switched it on.

Immediately, it let out a tuneful chime.

The voice message was from Crouch.

"Hey, not sure when you will land but we're based in Kingston at the Ocean Suites. Something's come up. We're heading out right now, but will contact when finished."

Crouch hung up. Alicia half-expected him to end with the word "over", as if talking through a radio, but that was the way with Crouch. Still associated with and happy to be living in his old SAS world. He was a sentimentalist at heart, and held the past dear. She sighed.

What now?

Instead of jumping right in, which was what she wanted to do, it looked like she was going to have to kick her heels for a while. Crouch hadn't said where the team were headed or when they'd be back. Alicia decided to head over to the Ocean

View and see if anything developed from there. She exited the terminal and jumped into a cab, took the ride into town and then around the outskirts. Kingston itself appeared to be an odd mix of everything she'd expected.

As she climbed out of the cab and paid the driver, her cellphone rang. *Great timing, Crouch,* she thought and basked for a moment in the direct sunlight before looking at her screen.

It wasn't Crouch. It was Healey, the youngest member of their team. Alicia immediately brushed off a trickle of ice water that started to seep down her spine. Healey never rang her. Why would...

"Yeah? What's up?" she answered quickly.

"Alicia? That you?"

The boy sounded panicked.

"Nappy stuck again?"

"No. *Listen.* Whoa, wait."

Alicia tried to pick through the words and inflections. Despite her ribbing, Healey was a soldier and a highly capable, if inexperienced, member of their team. It sounded like he was running.

"We followed a lead. Took a gamble. No danger to be seen but we knew something was hanging back just around the fringes of this thing."

Healey spoke in bursts as he ran and in quiet tones. Alicia didn't interrupt, she needed as much information as she could get.

"They must have been watching us. Maybe even a false lead, a lure. Brought us out here and then pounced. They got Russo, Alicia. And Crouch. Caitlyn too. I'm—"

Now Alicia was highly focused, preparing her mind for what was to come next as Healey paused again.

"Are they still chasing you?"

"Yeah. But I think . . . I think I'm clear. Wait."

Alicia waited, her every instinct straining like lions on a leash, determined and impatient to go to the aid of her colleagues.

"Okay, it's all focused around this treasure they say has never been found. Captain Morgan's loot. It started with the five ships found off Panama, which some now say aren't his ships at all and others say are the lesser spoils of his fleet."

"Where are you?"

"I'm trying to get coordinates as we speak."

Good job, Healey.

"They think the ships might contain little treasure and mostly bottles of rum. Which is why the brand named after the pirate are sponsoring the search. It would be great publicity for them. But it seems we've stepped on the toes of some big criminal outfit. Something's off about the whole thing, Alicia. Something's very off."

"How long ago did this go down?"

"Minutes. We're still—" Healey went quiet.

Alicia listened through the connection, wishing with everything she had that the lad would get the bloody coordinates over.

"All right, they're gone. I think I'm safe. And yeah, if the five ships hold no treasure why are these assholes all over it? It can't be about the rum, surely."

*Everything's about the rum,* Alicia thought in a moment of lighter consideration.

"The coordinates?" she asked.

"Yeah, here you go."

Healey grunted, and she heard a man's gruff voice, a shout and the sounds of a scuffle. Alicia felt her body go rigid, her fists clenching. Powerless to help, she listened as men set about her friend and colleague, the man she'd fought alongside in the field.

She could only hope for the best.

Healey cried out as a blow landed, then hit back. A man yelled and the entire melee became a jumble of blows and curse words. Alicia's heart leapt when someone shouted: "Shit, don't let the bastard get away!" Then noises of jogging and heavy breathing and a sudden groan from Healey.

A shout: "Got him!"

Alicia's heart sank.

More wrestling sounds and a few cries from unknown voices spanned the next few seconds. Then Healey groaned and she could almost see him beaten on the floor.

Somebody said: "His phone. Grab it and take it to the boss."

"I'll get the phone. You grab his legs."

"Shit. Bastard ran a long way, man. That's a long way back."

"Hey, that's the job."

"You think we'll get something out of him?"

"Dunno, man. Easier him than the big dude and the old guy. Even the woman looks tougher than this kid."

Alicia felt the strain in her knuckles as her fists clenched even harder.

"He's connected here," another voice, "talking to someone."

"You're fucking kidding me. Bring it here."

Alicia felt her eyes close in despair. Healey was down. The crew captured. Location unknown. Could a computer whiz track the call? Did she have access to one in Jamaica? Shit, there just wasn't enough *time*.

"Whoever you are," hushed vehement tones spoke down the phone line, "you'd best prepare four caskets. Five, if you're planning on joining us."

And then laughter. Vicious laughter. Alicia listened as the man turned the phone off. The prospects of finding a hidden fortune always brought out the worst. Today was no exception.

Alicia would never give in though. Time was her enemy, but

all else could be fought and fought until even the last shred of hope was gone. She held the phone away from her ear, checked the screen.

Thank fuck for that.

A text message had been received.

It displayed the coordinates to Healey's location.

She prayed she could make it in time.

## CHAPTER THREE

Alicia exploded into a flurry of action. The coordinates, when entered into an app on her cellphone, pointed toward Montego Bay, on the opposite side of the bloody island. Hours to drive it.

Alicia processed it all in just a few moments. Her soldier's mind wanted to fight, to strike out; the old impulses hard to quell. But this was a highly unusual situation. She couldn't remember the last time she'd had to face something like this alone.

And alone she was.

You didn't trust the locals in an unknown city, and her own team were too far away. In short then, there was only one option. Alicia flagged down another cab and took it all the way back to the airport. She used her other team's SPEAR credentials, approved at the highest level by the US government, to finesse access to the private hangers and runways and took a quick wander around. The sun glared, the hubbub clamored at her, the sweat popped across her brow and shoulders, but nothing broke her focus. In the end there were only two real possibilities.

Alicia studied them closely. The one she chose was just that bit younger, that bit greener, that bit more . . . likely.

"Hey, I need your help."

"Ma'am," the young chopper pilot said. "Is there a problem?"

"Oh yeah. You call me ma'am again and I'll box your friggin' ears."

The pilot looked blank. "Excuse me?"

"Look mate—" she moved beside him and put an arm gently around his shoulders "—the powers-that-be say I have to go to Montego Bay. They say now. I'd be willing to throw a little extra at the flyboy that helps me out. Whaddya say?"

Alicia took out her wallet.

The pilot blinked. "Oh, I can't. I—"

"Yeah," Alicia flapped the wallet as if it was a winning lottery ticket. "You can."

The man's eyes were hungry.

Alicia let him see the wadded notes. "An hour there. An hour back. Easy money."

"Well, it's a bit more than that."

"But you get my company too." Alicia gave him the wide-eyed grin. "That's gotta be worth something."

"Oh, of course." The pilot was nothing if not polite. "I didn't mean anything by that."

"Hey, loosen up." Alicia gave him a friendly punch on the arm. "Sorry, hope that doesn't bruise up too much." She saw the uncertainty in his eyes and tried another tack.

"I wonder if that other guy over there could help me."

A minute later and their deal was done. The pilot's name was James and, despite his nervousness and clear reluctance, he soon had the ultra-modern bird in the air. A quick flight plan had been filed and Alicia was heading toward Healey's last coordinates—the port at Montego Bay. For the first time she began to feel a little lighter—she was on her way to help her friends and less than an hour had passed. The sun outside was inching down the horizon, the heat slowly fading, but that was good too. Alicia preferred to arrive with the shadows.

Which also brought her back around to the situation she was approaching. Alicia had no weapons and no knowledge of the area save for what she could scavenge from the Internet. It appeared to be a relatively flat and open port, one side tasked to the docking of boats and the other a jumble of containers. At least one large gantry crane ran up and down one side. Alicia saw no real cover apart from the containers themselves, but still couldn't put her trust totally into the hands of a map app.

James tried to make small talk as they skimmed beneath the clouds. "So what do you do over in Montego Bay? PR?"

Alicia almost chortled, but managed to stop herself at the very last moment. "You think I'd be good at PR?"

"I do. You have all the right moves, miss."

Was that a little bit of flirting? Alicia missed those days—hadn't seen them in so long she'd forgotten how it went. She managed to curb the crudity that was about to slip from her mouth and turned it into a half-true comment.

"My company needs me. Help them out of a bind."

James nodded. "Well, settle back. We're an hour out."

Alicia nodded and began to prepare.

The chopper started to dip, then glide down. Alicia steadied her thoughts and imagined the possible outcomes. She combed her memory, ran through ideas. She fixed the main objectives firmly at the forefront of her mind.

Crouch. Russo. Caitlyn. Healey.

James landed sweetly and took his money with a grin, more confident now that his risks were over. Alicia considered inviting him on the next leg of her mission, but only for a private joke. It wouldn't be right, and she was trying to change.

She made her way to the port of Montego Bay, stepping out of a cab near the entrance and into the shadow of the biggest cruise ship she'd ever seen. The area behind her along the dock was a hive of motion, too many bodies moving to get a bead on any one person. The area before her, however, as the dock turned more industrialized and less public, appeared almost deserted.

Alicia scanned the horizons. The sun was slipping low. Shadows were seeping free. It had been a very long day.

She had no weapons. But she didn't need one.

Alicia Myles *was* the weapon.

## CHAPTER FOUR

Alicia used her cellphone to pinpoint Healey's exact location. Of course, the altercations must have happened in broad daylight, but she fancied a determined force might just get away with it. Barring gunshots, the commotion and sheer noise around the busy dockside would mask an awful lot of sound. A walk around the perimeter revealed relatively easy access to the place, and minimal security. The security office looked unmanned. Alicia began to wonder if this area might be a private storage facility.

Readying herself, she walked inside.

Soon among the containers and feeling safer. CCTV cameras were mounted on poles at all four sides of the compound, but if they were anything like the security office then they wouldn't pose a problem. Of course, the criminal element might be using them—they'd be somewhat lax not to. But maybe they were obsolete. Alicia could only hope.

It took her twenty minutes to find the place where Healey had sent his text. Hundreds of containers surrounded her. No noise penetrated what felt like a metal maze, a blinding-hot partitioned box. She searched the area but found nothing save boot prints and what appeared to be dried blood.

Healey? Where are you? Show me a sign now.

Time ticked and stretched out, the waiting part of her journey now at an end. This was where she could act. This was where she could make a difference. But short of getting herself noticed and potentially in the same boat as her teammates, what the hell was she supposed to do?

Time still spilled away faster than sand through fingers. What state were her friends in by now? How long could they withstand the pressure? Were they even now sat inside one of these metal boxes, wasted, dehydrated, just wishing for help to arrive?

Alicia began to think more desperate alternatives as darkness appropriated the land.

For fuck's sake, guys, do something!

## CHAPTER FIVE

Zack Healey stayed as hard-faced as he could, as resolute as an ancient forest tree. Still, the men interrogating him knew his rawness. It seemed they could smell it seeping from his pores.

The fist landed again, smashing his head to the side. Healey felt an explosion of pain and the metallic taste of blood filling his mouth. He knew about this though, knew how to fight it. The training had been much harder. The British soldier had to be ready for anything. Healey had figured at the moment of his capture that it was he that would be leaned upon. Didn't take a genius to figure he was the weak link.

"Speak," his aggressor growled.

"The more you hit my face, the less I can," he replied.

Another punch.

Healey took it. Behind, he heard Caitlyn stifle a cry and just wished she'd remain quiet. The more low-key her presence the better. These guys clearly believed she was a civilian along for the ride, maybe a consultant, and believed she wouldn't be privy to the more sensitive information that they were after. *Fine. Let them think that. Let them think that and keep on hitting me. Because if they hurt her...*

Healey looked up from the floor as a new voice made itself heard.

"Wait. For now. The boy is right." It was a grating, highly accented voice, something eastern European.

Healey looked up. "Boy?"

"Ah, you have to see enough things to become a man. I feel you have not seen these things yet. But who knows? You do not know me and I do not know you. Not yet. Let's change that a little, shall we?"

Healey just stared at the man, grateful for the respite for now. His jaw throbbed, his teeth ached.

"I am Jake. You call me Jake."

Healey shuffled in his chair, but couldn't go far. The legs were nailed to the ground, the arms colored with old blood. A regular questioning point, this then. A go-to method. Healey couldn't think of any use of that knowledge, but then he usually left the real thinking to the others.

Men sat around, or idled with their backs against the metal sides of the box. A passable air-conditioner cooled the inside, and bottles of water were passed around. Healey longed for a swig but didn't let them know.

"What are you looking for? What have you found? Why are you here? Are there more of you? C'mon, man, just answer me one for now."

*Vague questions,* Healey thought. Of course the main boss would be questioning Crouch. These were underlings, allowed to play.

"We came here to view the yard," Healey told him. "To rent a container."

"You can't do that, man. Containers belong to shipping company."

Healey spread a palm as best he could. "But clearly you can."

"Who's your contact?"

Healey ran through the information they'd picked up just before setting off on this ill-fated exercise. Crouch was the kind of man that kept a contact in every city—every *port* as it were. Upon arrival in Jamaica he had sent out the feelers then sat back and waited for the hits to come in. Anything connected with the incredible find or the treasure they'd already hauled up. Anything revolving around Captain Henry Morgan or the people that were involved in the search. Trees shook. Calls were placed. Dirty money smeared across greasy palms. In the end, a trickle of information and then a hot tip had come in. An informant would meet them at the Montego Bay port...

And here they were.

Clearly, the criminal element was high and invested in some kind of enterprise. The bad news for them was—Crouch and his crew now knew.

"We don't have any contact," Healey said, for want of saying something different. "Clearly you guys have your ears to the ground. You should know."

The man in charge frowned as if struggling to understand Healey's turn of phrase. "You came here for a reason though, didn't you? How about you tell me why."

Healey realized he should probably have kept quiet. These situations always ended up with a question he couldn't handle. He wondered just how far they'd take it. He'd already tested his bonds and the ties were secure. Not unbreakable given the right moment, but the pain was going to have to be worth the payoff.

"Maybe you should ask the girl," one of the guys said.

Healey stiffened immediately, a movement not unnoticed by Jake, who shrugged. "Is she your girlfriend?"

Healey stayed quiet. There was no good end to these questions.

"Bring her here," Jake drawled.

Healey turned as best he could in the chair, torn between a need to protect Caitlyn Nash and the knowledge that he should remain impassive. Caitlyn was a strong woman, she'd fought through her fair share of tragedy, but a volatile situation like this should be avoided.

"Tell me," Jake said softly as Caitlyn was propelled forward and deposited in a wooden chair next to Healey. "We won't be taking silence for an answer."

Healey tried not to look at Caitlyn, more conscious than ever now of his feelings for his colleague. They walked these dangerous paths every day; they knew the potential outcomes of every mission. But sometimes . . . just sometimes . . . a desperate situation really drove it home.

"We're here to rent," Caitlyn backed Healey's words up, hollow though they were. "Just a container or two."

Jake let out a breath and checked his watch. "Boss gave us a couple hours with you two. We're stepping it up."

He nodded at an underling who stepped forward, fists bunched. Healey saw his intentions in an instant and tried to jump up.

"No!"

"We don't want to do this," Jake said.

"Let her be!" Healey wrenched at his bonds, struggling hard. The chair rocked a little, fighting its bolts. Men rose all around the container.

"You can shout all you want," Jake said. "Nobody gonna hear you, man."

"She doesn't know anything!"

"We know you're searching for the treasure under the Panama Sea. We know that. You tell us the rest and we'll lay off."

Healey spluttered. The man cuffed Caitlyn, not hard but enough to snap her head to the right; her eyes suddenly locked on Healey's and wide with fear. The young soldier jerked hard at his bonds.

Jake stepped in, took Healey's face and squeezed. "Why you here, man?"

He had faced down much worse, but not with the woman he loved captured beside him. Worst case scenarios and stomach churning outcomes sprang out from the dark corners of his mind, all twisting and writhing in the few moments he had to choose. The world suddenly became a much darker place.

"We're treasure hunters," he said softly. "She's my friend. Don't hurt her again."

"All right." Jake grinned, spreading his hands. "But we already knew that. How 'bout you tell me more?"

Healey tried to calm himself. The soldier had withdrawn, replaced by the man, the lover. Caitlyn was his first. In some ways, the experience of life was just beginning.

"We are a team of investigators—" finessing the truth "—seeking out old artifacts, lost treasure, ancient relics, that kind of thing. We found Aztec gold in the US, crusaders' gold in the UK, and missed out on a few other finds." He drew it out for more time. "We followed more than a few red herrings of late. Peru. France. Failure puts us back but doesn't deter us. We knew about this find . . . these five ships . . . but nothing ever came of it."

Jake whistled. "Phew, listen to him now. More words than a dictionary."

"What else do you need?"

"You told me nothin' yet, man."

"This is our job. We're not chasing you or your organization. We just crossed paths by chance."

Jake glanced over at Caitlyn.

Healey rushed on, "Captain Henry Morgan. Lost five ships off Panama, most of which were believed to be loaded down with loot. This because by the time Morgan reached Panama he was already tremendously wealthy. Where else could he store his riches? He wouldn't bank it. Wouldn't leave it behind. But—" Healey smiled "—in relation to that line of thinking, would he really put it all on his ships for his pirate brethren to watch over?"

Jake shrugged. "Dunno, man. Would he?"

"Well, maybe. It had to be transported sometime, right? But

those five ships were found years ago. One was believed to be Morgan's flagship—the *Satisfaction*. Still no proof and no treasure has been found. But . . ." Healey paused as he heard a noise.

"But what?" Jake urged him on.

"But maybe they found . . . something."

## CHAPTER SIX

Rob Russo was a big man, a broad, chunky muscle-bound figure with a rock-hard presence and a head like a boulder. The physical presence couldn't be altered, but the man beneath was entirely interchangeable. Russo was a first-class soldier, through and through, but had a deep, caring heart and a personable nature.

Once you got to know him.

The container that was his jail cell echoed to a chorus of malicious cheering.

Russo's captives, instead of questioning him, had each decided to fight him. Russo stood at the center of the container, a large man covered in tattoos snuffling in his face like a fierce bull. A haymaker missed him by an inch. Russo backed away. Men cheered and laughed around him, eight of them. Russo wished the number was a little less, he could probably have taken them out. But eight in such a tight space? No chance. The bull came in again, roaring this time. Russo took a blow to the chest so the man opened himself up, then came down hard with elbows and a knee to the stomach. Bull-Face fell to one knee.

Russo hesitated.

A mistake he rarely made, but worry for his fellow captives and their unknown fates played havoc with his senses. Bull-Face drove up off one knee, striking Russo under the chin and sending him reeling. Russo struck the back of the container with a loud bang, but the attack brought some clarity. Russo saw the bull charging again, sidestepped rather niftily for a man his size and helped the running bulk on its way. The bull struck the metal solidly, face-first, and slithered slowly to the floor.

Russo turned to face the man who'd been talking. "There's no point to this. Nobody wins."

"Are you not having fun, big lad? We are. It's not often we get a big lad to play with. This is what we do. Day an' night. Don't worry 'bout hittin' hard."

The next in line stepped up, a scrawny rake with hard knots for muscles. Stripped to the waist, his body bore bruises both new and old, attesting heavily to these men's pastimes. He came at Russo instantly and hard, not caring about taking a hit and trying to bring the big man down with some well-placed nerve-cluster shots. Russo was aware of them all, striking back in a similar manner. The two circled each other like wary animals until the sound of a phone ringing distracted the leader.

"Shit, that'll be Jensen."

Men grinned as if admitting they'd gotten a little distracted, but the leader was clearly worried. "Just keep it down. Hello?"

"What have you got?"

"Umm, nothing yet, boss. Guy's tighter than a zip tie." A grin at his men for thinking fast.

"Then what's all the noise for?"

"Ah..."

Russo chose that moment to roar loudly and take the scrawny man down, using the element of surprise without guilt, knocking him out with a single punch to the right temple. As if in answer, Jensen's voce roared out of the open cell.

"Stop fucking around, Holmes, and get me some answers!"

Holmes spent another few minutes apologizing and then turned a red face to Russo. "Get him tied down. We have to go to work."

Russo evaluated the situation. Seven against one. Was it worth a shot? Was it worth risking potential broken bones now or waiting for a better chance later? It was always hard to pass an opportunity by when your life might depend on it.

Fight now? Or later?

He heard noises outside the container and wondered if anyone else might be abroad tonight. There was always that chance. He might not see eye to eye with the inimitable Alicia Myles, but he'd follow her into any battle. She would always have his back.

There was just a chance that she might make it.

Russo sat himself down in the chair.

## CHAPTER SEVEN

Michael Crouch had known some perilous situations in his time and counted this among them. He saw no way—and certainly no sign—that these opportunistic bandits would let them go.

Their leader, a man who'd introduced himself as John Jensen, had been questioning Crouch on and off for some time now, his attempts hindered by phone call after phone call and some hard decision making.

Now he put the phone down once more, shaking his head. "A crew mostly made up of idiots and losers," he said. "But with an inherited crew you have to work with what you got. Am I right?"

Crouch nodded agreeably. "I guess so." Talking always helped prolong these situations and the more they spun it out, the more chance there was of the bad guys losing control.

"We think you're the leader. We think you know the most. Let's start with those five ships, Mr. Crouch, and go from there."

Crouch gritted his teeth, just managing to refrain from shaking his head. Of all the weirdness surrounding this case, meeting an old colleague had to be near the top of the pile. John Jensen was tall and brawny, with just a scrubbing of bristle covering the top of his head. He was also ex-SAS, and a good solider in his day, a man Crouch had brushed shoulders with but never commanded. The shock of their meeting was still fresh.

"You didn't leave under a cloud. What happened?"

Jensen evaluated him. "You know, I never slipped under any cloud. Not once. And I never made anything for myself either.

Not once. About a decade ago I put two and two together and decided to see what I could make with what little I had. Turned out—" he spread his arms "—we're still waiting to see."

"That's a little vague, to be honest."

"Oh, sorry. So sorry. I really thought I was the one asking the questions here. You're a treasure hunter, right, Crouch? Always was. I'm similar, only in a nastier way."

"I waited until after retirement to pursue my dream."

Jensen shrugged. "Retirement'll get you killed quickly, mate. If you love life you don't stop living it."

Crouch studied the man whom he gauged to be in his late forties, early fifties. In some ways he reminded him of a few old pupils. There were flashes of Matt Drake, his friend and prodigy, others too, but of course all these men were trained the same. Similarities had to exist.

Jensen reached out a hand so that it could be filled with a glass of alcohol. "You know," he said, swigging it down and wiping his mouth, "the pirates of old, they supposedly didn't bury their treasure. So a hundred *experts* tell us. But I say take your bloody experts and make 'em walk the damn plank."

Jensen was grinning now, playing it up, swigging the alcohol and waving the glass around. And though he was smiling, Crouch fancied he saw a mad glint deep down inside those Caribbean blue eyes, a madness buried deep.

"Oh, don't worry." Jensen laughed. "It's not that I really do think I'm a pirate. But we've been pillaging these shores for nigh on half a decade now. It's hard not to identify."

Crouch drew a breath. They were all in deeper trouble than he'd realized. And the truth was, he did know a little more than the others.

"So, let me start you off, old boy." Jensen held the glass out for a refill. "Henry Morgan and his band of brigands sack Panama. Their ships sink. Fast forward to a few years ago and they're found but so deeply entombed they might never be opened. A process they call carbonate concretion. So far, they've got into one. I'm sure you know that. A further complication exists with the Lajas Reef. Many ships have crashed into it and sunk over the years, so it becomes even harder to pick them apart. So far all they've discovered is a bunch of old cannons and a few lead seals. Hardly treasure now, is it?"

Crouch nodded. "I agree. But efforts are continuing. Perhaps they will bring up something useful soon."

Jensen raised a brow. "Or perhaps they already have."

Crouch felt some trepidation. "What makes you think that?"

Jensen rose. "It's been five hundred years, Michael. Morgan's treasure is still out there somewhere, never found. Still sitting in its iron-bound chest. Still waiting for that day . . ." Jensen pretended to pluck something from the air.

Crouch sighed. "Thoughts like that can send a man mad."

Jensen punched him right in the face. "Ya think?"

"I do now." Crouch reached up to rub his jaw, thankful his wrists hadn't been tied.

"This is where it gets tough, Crouch. I've been a little lenient up to now for old time's sake, but this . . . this is a tricky situation for you. I need to know what you know right now."

Crouch looked across at the man he'd been captured with. Named Leno, he was a local of sorts, a diver that plied his trade all across the region. Of course, there were good pickings around and good money to be made in the sparkling waters of the Caribbean. Leno, though, was the kind of diver that liked to supplement his income.

"You've seen what he brought to us. I just finished going over them myself when you turned up. They're a bunch of treasure maps found alongside the seals and swords. Leno spirited them away for profit."

"When you say treasure maps . . ." Jensen glanced over at the sheaf of papers Leno attested were from the sunken ship and had been protected by some kind of leather and tarpaulin pouch.

"Well, not in the Hollywood sense," Crouch said. "But I'm sure you know this is about as close as it gets."

"I guess."

Leno had made no movement or sound until now, but looked up when he felt Jensen's eyes upon him.

"Tell me now. These are from Morgan's ship? And you took them to do what with? Sell to the highest bidder?"

Leno nodded miserably.

"And why would that bidder be this man?"

"We have backing," Crouch immediately jumped to Leno's aid. "A man with great resources who wants ancient treasures to go back to their rightful owners."

"Oh, how nice, a rich man with nothing else to do. I get it. Hard to say who those 'rightful owners' would be though, don't you think? Such a corrupt world these days."

"Nothing changes, not really," Crouch said. "We just think we're advancing."

Jensen looked over at Crouch as if he were suddenly in a different world.

## CHAPTER EIGHT

John Jensen hid it well, but fancied that his humanity might be gone. Hardship and ill-living, dark thoughts and bottles of rum had stripped away whatever light veneer of compassion he'd once had, leaving a living shell of greed and decadence behind.

He knew it, but the knowledge seemed to have diluted in intensity over the years. Jensen was a pirate now, plying these fair shores for whatever bounty he could carry off. The old days were gone—the hours of watching and waiting for the enemy, the endless days of following orders and jumping from one dangerous den of vipers to the next.

Now, he was the viper. And he knew how to stay under the radar.

The raids had started low-key, nothing more than daylight robberies and midnight break-ins. He'd made his way, paid for it with the belongings of others. It was a different life, lived in peace and under a wonderful sky with such peaceful waters nearby always ready to help with the cleansing. Petty crime had led to bigger stuff, and when he started to apply his military training to problems and new concepts an exciting new world showed the potential of opening up.

Men came along, recruited from bars at first and then by word of mouth. Jensen achieved a small reputation and then some good men. Things moved on. They targeted lone boats and well-guarded properties. They leaned on influential people who had secrets to keep. Jensen learned the art of leverage. He founded a base, tailored himself after a seventeenth century pirate or two. As a group they even began to search the old wrecks for sunken treasure, finding very little but occasionally coming home with a bagful of doubloons. The things that lay on the ocean floor fascinated Jensen. He knew of shipwrecks that might be worth millions.

It had come as a bit of a shock when Henry Morgan's name had come up. Of course he knew about the five ships. Of course he knew the legends. But there were thousands of wrecks at the bottom of the sea. Could there really be a new hoard in his own backyard?

Well, strictly—no.

Jensen watched both Crouch and Leno, trusting them less than he trusted most of his own men. His three lieutenants, Labadee and Forrester were his first and second mates, with Levy coming a close third. If he trusted anyone at all it was these three. They had been there from the beginning.

Jensen let his mind wander a little. Their current workload was heavy, made up of small jobs across many islands, but everything paled in comparison to finding such a treasure hoard. It was nothing short of a life's dream. *All resources, all in.* Jensen had built up a solid network of spies, snitches and well-placed informants through the years. Now he could reap the rewards of such judicious planning. And truth be told, he didn't care too much for Crouch and his cronies. Didn't care how they ended up. All he wanted to wring from them was information.

The time to talk was almost at an end.

Truth be told, in his younger days he'd been a little in awe of Michael Crouch. But then so had everyone. Even an outfit as professional and superior as the SAS loved to talk. The whispers were that Crouch had started a covert splinter division, and that they were kicking some major European ass. All good, but that and a few other victories sent Crouch's reputation toward the stratosphere. And now Jensen knew how this crew had been able to move forward so quickly and efficiently.

Crouch was better connected than Vodafone.

Still, he moved alone these days. Part of this crew. Jensen very much doubted anyone in authority would know where he was. It was time to move things along.

"It was good to see you again, Michael."

He raised a gun.

## CHAPTER NINE

Alicia Myles never stood on ceremony nor backed down, and a night like this was hardly about to make her change her ways. A rap on the door of the container and a wrench of the handles brought a shaven head into view which she promptly introduced to a piece of broken metal she'd found just outside. When the head went down hard she found the shoulders and hauled out the rest of the body. Then she took its place.

Inside the door of the container she glared straight at Rob Russo.

"Crap, Myles, where the hell have you been?"

"Tanning. You?"

"Fighting. Wanna help?"

"Ooh, now you're just teasing."

Alicia sidestepped a lunging man, whipped the length of metal up and made contact with his head. He spun away, bleeding. She whirled the piece again, one skull, then another, leaving the men dazed in her wake. Russo bear-hugged a man into unconsciousness.

"Stop cuddling them and start hitting," Alicia hissed. "No wonder you're still a prisoner. Or . . ."

She paused as a man flew at her, then she spun on the spot and hefted him over a shoulder.

"Maybe you enjoy the manly contact?" she finished.

Russo finished the groaning man off. "Stop talking, Myles. The shit that comes out of your mouth could bury a cruise ship."

Alicia met the next man head on, surprising him with her

strength and speed. His blows were deflected, his arms bruised. She ended up breaking the metal spar across his skull and then stared down at the damaged pieces,

"Bollocks."

Russo engaged the three men she'd already injured whilst another two confronted her. It seemed they'd learned their lesson as they came at once, fists flying. Alicia danced away but the area was tiny, leaving her nowhere to go. These men loved a fistfight, though. Alicia had counted on it—their guns had been left at the sides of the container. She bobbed and weaved, took a punch to the jaw and gave one back. Russo heaved one of his adversaries atop the other, and now there was a smile on his face.

Alicia echoed it.

"Come closer, boys. Let's see what you've got."

They leapt impetuously. Alicia was already sidestepping away. Three lightning fast jabs into nerve clusters doubled them over. The first she then sent smashing into the metal wall, an impact that dented the surface. The second she spun around and finished off with several more jabs, all faster than he could breathe.

He went down beside his friend, out cold.

Alicia turned to Russo, and saw him dealing with the two remaining, almost comatose, adversaries.

"Take your time," she muttered and walked past, leaving him to finish. Outside, the air was balmy and the night relatively quiet; only a few thuds and quiet laughter from the nearby container that housed Healey and Caitlyn. Alicia angled her walk toward it, knowing those inside wouldn't be as lax as Russo's captors and Healey might not be in a position to help.

Russo bounded up, panting.

"Good dog," Alicia said. "Finish your bones? There's a good boy. Now get serious for a minute will you?"

Russo was caught between glaring and indignity, unable to think of a single thing to say.

"Jeez, you take a hit back there? Scramble what few brains ya got left? Now listen—they have Healey and Caitlyn in here. Healey's been taking some damage. You ready?"

Russo held up two guns and two knives he'd taken from his own container. "Yeah, Myles. Are you?"

Alicia took her weapons without comment, then rubbed sharply at the place where one of the bruisers had socked her in the jaw. In her line of work such an injury wasn't unusual but she wished more than a day or two could go by between the knocks.

"Ready?"

"Ready."

Alicia wrenched the bars that opened the doors and Russo barreled his way inside. Her first view was of his back and then the square box opened up to her eyes. Men stared in shock from various positions around the walls. Several were seated, caught out. A younger man standing by the only table in the room reached for one of the guns that lay there, but Russo shot him. Alicia opened fire and took down another. Her eyes happened upon a rifle that lay next to another handgun, confirming the remainder of a plan she'd been hatching in her mind. No time for that now though. Men flew at her from the edges of the container.

Healey's head was hanging, a ribbon of blood pooling onto the floor at his feet. Caitlyn stared fixedly, unharmed, but almost unable to believe help had arrived in time to save them. Alicia willed her to remain as still as possible.

She remained close to the table, not allowing anyone to get past her and reach the weapons. A knife-wielder slashed at her throat but Alicia managed to fend him off, using her own blade to take him down. A man then flung himself at her, causing a wild back-peddle. She crashed into the table itself which broke under the impact, all four legs shattering and breaking away. Handguns tumbled and the rifle slithered to the side. Alicia dropped her knife but picked up one of the table legs and battered her opponent across the face. He rolled away, groaning. She jumped on him, then saw a blur rush by to her right, spun again and snagged the man's legs just as he reached down for a weapon,

Desperate, she tugged his ankles, dragging him away.

It was a chaotic fray, reminiscent of a schoolyard scrap but much more dangerous. Alicia battered at both men with the table leg, then jumped atop the second man who was closest to the guns. A compact jab to the back of the neck took the fight out of him.

Russo tackled three, the soldier clearly knowing it was important to thin the herd as early as possible. One he shot, the other he collided with head on. Then he tripped but held on to the gun, firing upward as a man descended on him with a machete.

Machete!

The weapon sent even Russo's blood boiling. Luckily said weapon only clattered to about an inch away from him, useless as its wielder collapsed dead on the floor. Before Russo sat Healey and Caitlyn, and beyond that Alicia still struggled. Another enemy figure stood close to Healey.

Alicia sat up and took a bead on the last man standing.

"Stand back, asshole."

"Name's Mike. What's yours?"

"Stand the fuck away."

Mike turned a little so that Alicia could see the bright blade he held poised at Healey's neck. "Say what?"

Alicia picked up a gun and aimed it in a single movement. Russo made it clear he was also holding one. Mike merely grinned. "You want to save this kid. You let me go."

Alicia saw the blade had already drawn a streak of red. "Stop."

"Put your guns down. Let me walk."

Alicia knew it would be straight to the next container for backup.

"Put the blade down and we'll let you walk."

"You hurt him, you die," Russo added. "Only way out is to comply."

Mike struggled visibly with it, torn between wanting to be anywhere but here and signaling his crew. The odds were not good and he clearly knew it. Alicia let him sweat, knowing the more he wavered the less sharp he'd be when the time came. As he vacillated Caitlyn stared Healey right in the eyes.

"He's also playing for time," she said.

Alicia tightened her grip on the gun. Mike flexed the muscles of his arm, blade about to dig deeper, but then Healey himself rose up, ties breaking, pulling away from the blade and swiping at Mike's face. Shocked, the merc tried to lunge forward, knife wavering. As soon as the tiniest gap opened up, Alicia fired. Mike fell away, groaning, the knife clattering to the floor. He made a quick lunge but Alicia jumped in hard with blows to the abdomen. Mike's forehead cracked the floor as he fell asleep.

Alicia met Healey's wide eyes. "You okay?"

"Yeah, yeah. Just give me a sec."

"Thought you were gonna sit there all day," she said airily.

Healey regarded her as if seeing her for the first time. "You kidding?"

"Do they still have Michael?" Caitlyn asked, although the answer was clearly obvious.

"Yep," Alicia said. "I've rescued three quarters of you. Thought I'd save the boss till last."

"Oh shit, we're never going to hear the end of it," Russo moaned.

"Damn right." Alicia grinned.

"Hey, Myles, if it was up to you," Russo blustered. "Poor ole Healey would still be sitting there."

"Hey . . ."

"No time," Caitlyn said.

Russo jumped for the rifle.

## CHAPTER TEN

Alicia hurried through the weapons and handed the best suited to Healey and Caitlyn. The researcher of the team knew how to hold and use a handgun, and had a few combat skills since Healey decided she needed to know at least enough to keep her alive. *Well done, Zack,* Alicia thought. That was some fine forward thinking. Together, the three of them rushed out of the open container doors and back into the night.

The first thing Alicia felt was a welcome breeze on her face and a lifting of the cloying heat that had settled over them all despite the rudimentary air conditioning. The second thing she saw was the nearby container doors slamming open and four men rushing out. They held rifles with attached sights and camo jackets. Alicia lined them up, staying out in the open.

"First to move is target practice," she said easily.

The four men spread out, covered now by Healey and Caitlyn too. Alicia could almost smell the fear washing off Caitlyn but a quick glance revealed no clear presence of it. *Good.* Alicia gave Caitlyn a reassuring nod.

Next out of the container came Crouch, a scared-looking stranger, two more thugs, and a man with the air of a leader. Not least because he still held a glass of dark liquid in one hand.

"Well, well," he said. "There's another one of you."

Alicia couldn't help but stare. Despite his well-bred accent this man had an air, an aura that reminded her of her boyfriend. And the way he carried himself, the steely blue eyes and confident gait. She was pretty sure he was military, if not the SAS. But he showed no obvious signs of recognition.

"Michael," she said, exuding a confidence of her own. "I'm assuming the scared guy there is your contact?"

Their boss nodded quickly, giving no names away but helping Alicia decide who exactly belonged in the enemy camp.

"John Jensen," the leader of the crew offered and raised his glass. "Good night for it, eh?"

Another bloody crackpot, Alicia thought. Is the world so full of them?

"Hand him over," she said, "and we all live to fight another day."

Jensen nodded agreeably. "Sure, sure. We'll get to that. Michael here was just telling me about your little quest."

Alicia grunted. "Well, lucky you. That's more than he told me. I just got here."

Jensen laughed. "Very good. But, look, I'm running out of rum here. Can we move matters along?"

"Sure. Where do you want the bullet?"

"Is Henry Morgan's treasure worth such violence?"

Alicia considered Jensen's actions of the night. He seemed to think so. A palpable air of tension hung over the scene, making the mercenaries itchy and sweat bleed into their eyes. It seemed there were only three people unaffected by it all: Alicia, Jensen and Crouch.

"The promise of wealth is such a great divider," Crouch said then, "and brings out the true colors of men and women, both the bright and the dark. How much wealth do you think you can amass before you are satisfied?"

Jensen lowered his glass. "Truly? Does there have to be a limit?"

His men guffawed. Alicia took a deep breath and steadied her aim. The knife edge tension deepened.

"Did you know that in England, Henry Morgan was known as one of the country's greatest naval tacticians? Whilst on the

Spanish Main he was known as a bloodthirsty pillager and liar. How differently history and distance can judge a man. How influential the scribes and papers can be, retelling only what they need for sensationalism. For sales." Jensen shrugged. "It's all relative to an agenda."

"Are you saying that you're misunderstood?" Alicia asked.

"Just tell me what you know. Then we can get on."

The night went silent; all breath was held. Jensen made no move but Alicia sensed the end was but a word away. She sent out a wish and then that wish was answered.

A bright red dot appeared on Jensen's vest, just above his heart.

The military man saw it instantly, eyes narrowing. He appeared to evaluate them once more. "How odd," he said. "I saw the appearance of a woman but missed the vanishing of a man."

"Rum will do that to you," Alicia said.

Jensen laughed shortly. "Not to me. I wrongly assumed he was behind a different container."

"So hand over Crouch. And we go away to fight another day. Or..."

She shrugged, indicating the top of the containers where Russo lay cradling the rifle. Jensen didn't hesitate, but turned to the leader of the Gold Team and bowed ever so slightly.

"Well done, Michael. This time. There will soon be another."

"I don't doubt it." Crouch stepped warily past Jensen and headed for Alicia. The blonde sidestepped carefully as he came to make sure she never dropped her rifle, nor lost her aim. Jensen made a show of clicking fingers at his men.

"Back off now," he said aloud.

Alicia followed suit slowly, with Healey and Caitlyn keeping their own sights up and Crouch leading the way. Carefully, they inched toward the deeper darkness.

"You have a car or something?" Healey whispered out of the corner of his mouth.

"Nope. Choppered in."

"Even better," Crouch said. "A safe, fast ride."

"Not really," Alicia said. "I sent the pilot back to Kingston."

"Bollocks."

"There's always the cruise ship," Caitlyn offered.

"Not if we want to stop this Jensen guy. That thing won't dock for a week."

"Hey, this is Montego Bay," Crouch said quietly. "There will be someone willing to drop everything and take us to Kingston. All we need is a wad of dollars. Leno, are you all right?"

Their contact, the diver that had stolen the maps, nodded bleakly. "For now."

"I'd take a long break, mate," Healey said. "Maybe head over to the US."

"Did you keep the maps?" Caitlyn asked Crouch as they continued to melt away, moving faster the further they went and presently joined by a panting Russo.

"Not a chance," Crouch said. "Jensen never let them out of his sight."

"What about—" Caitlyn tapped the side of her head.

"I saw all of them, remember most of them. But I need to get it all down on paper before it begins to fade."

Alicia didn't doubt that Crouch could remember much of what he'd seen. The man was one of the best trained military men on the planet, with one of the best Special Forces teams, and had been working at the highest level for most of his life. She'd trust his memory above almost all others.

At least, she'd always thought so until last week. Now wasn't the time but she would have to challenge Crouch over Beau's comments. And if the traitor was trying to cast a cloud over Crouch then the man needed to know. No telling how deep it went.

"I know a guy in Kingston," Crouch said unsurprisingly. "Maybe he can suggest someone in Montego Bay."

"Make it quick." Alicia eyed the shadows that crawled between containers. As the team walked further toward the light, the blackness at their backs became only more ominous. "My guess is Jensen's already pouring over those maps."

"So what's the plan?" Healey asked Crouch, already over his close ordeal.

"The plan?" Crouch smiled. "The plan never changes, my young friend. The plan will always be to locate the treasure before the other guy. So let's get started."

Crouch strode off in search of the nearest phone.

## CHAPTER ELEVEN

The journey back to Kingston was fast and silent, the team gathering themselves and getting over the peril they had just encountered. Alicia could have happily ribbed them all about it, but was conscious of the youth around her. Healey was a good soldier, getting better with experience, and Caitlyn was basically a researcher with skills, whom nobody had the time to properly train. Alicia herself was trying to change for the better, and that included causing less antagonism within the unit. Sometimes she struggled, but oft times she succeeded. Every victory felt that little bit better.

Kingston was a fast boat ride away, the motion and slam of the boat's hull guaranteed to send more than one of them green. Alicia had never been a great seafarer and clung on tightly until the ride was over. The team thanked their driver, paid the man his cash, and made their way back to the hotel.

Alicia sighed upon seeing it for the second time in less than twenty four hours. "God help them if they don't have any rooms."

"Well, you ain't bunking with me," Russo grumbled.

"Aw, Rob. You scared I'll steal all the bed covers, baby?"

"I'm scared you'll steal my *soul*."

"Ah, you missed your chance there. I snagged a guy already."

"Poor bastard."

Alicia inclined her head as they approached the hotel's front steps. "Now you know you don't mean that. I'm sure all the others don't too."

Russo shrugged as if not quite in agreement, but Alicia was

already pushing ahead into the gleaming lobby. Lights shone from all directions and it occurred to her then that she should probably have gotten a wash before trying to rent a room.

"Let's all head up to mine," Crouch said. "We should be able to book another by phone."

The elevator hummed its way up and still the team stayed quiet. Caitlyn was obviously itching to start the research, but Crouch and Alicia were just as eager to get back out into the field. Every lost minute put Jensen further ahead.

Crouch opened the door to his room and found bottles of water. Caitlyn managed a quick wash before heading over to the laptop. Healey studied his marked neck in the floor length mirror.

"Shit."

Alicia wandered up to him. "You're kidding, right? Looks more like a shaving cut."

"Har har."

"Oh, I see. No facial hair yet?"

"Alicia..."

She moved off after the warning, cooling her heels until Crouch finished writing down all he remembered of the maps, and Caitlyn found something useful on her computer. She found it hard to stop pacing, impossible to stop and sit. The training in her demanded action, not idleness, and the recent combat only raised her adrenalin.

"C'mon guys. Get a move on. Hey, Rob, wanna wrestle for money?"

Russo, cut out of the same cloth as Alicia, looked like he might be considering it. Then Caitlyn asked everyone to gather around. Alicia took a look out the window at the perfect Jamaican coastline, the dark outline of palm trees and the just visible rolling surf. Idyllic visions didn't suit her either, but just sometimes she wished they did.

"What do you have?" She approached Caitlyn.

"Henry Morgan's life. Recapping a few details, he amassed such a great fortune in a relatively short period. Nobody seems to know much about his youth, save that he spent it in Wales, UK, where his family owned a large farm that hasn't changed an awful lot since. Morgan grew up quite hard, it's believed, and came to Jamaica in 1658, marking himself as a man of valor. More used to weapons than literature, he took to the life of the seaman without issue. It appears he initially came to take part in Cromwell's plan to invade Hispaniola. His first command was in 1665."

"As a pirate?" Alicia wanted to know.

"He was never officially a pirate. England classed him a 'privateer', but who needs semantics? No, in 1665 he was still learning his trade. It appears when his captain was caught and executed by the Spanish, the crew elected Morgan as their leader."

"And so it began," Healey said, still gingerly touching his neck.

"Want me to bandage that for you?" Alicia tried to be thoughtful.

The young man blanched. "Um, no thanks. Have you even had medical training?"

"Bit of field strapping. Bit of under-fire triage. Hell, a neck's a neck, right? Just wrap something around it nice and tight."

Caitlyn was reading further ahead. "It appears Morgan fell into debt whilst partying in Jamaica's Port Royal. But he still had letters of marque from England, and was able to stay out at sea and pillage until the entire crew had enough to pay them off. They must have been bloody huge . . ." Caitlyn shook her head.

"What? Why?" Russo moved his huge head like a rotating stone statue.

"Well, they already had over fifty thousand pieces of eight

from the previous efforts. Now, they made the decision to strike at a city that harbored a considerable treasure. Porto Bello. And that's where Morgan's real pirating days begin."

At that moment, Crouch spoke up. "I have about as much written down as I can remember and some rudimentary drawings of coastlines. It's not great, but will have to do. And Leno did tell me that the maps were more about the writing anyway, not the sketches and steps from some landmark to another as more modern day works would have you believe. There is a big gap between how pirates were and what they did, and how they were then perceived after that one famous work of Robert Louis Stevenson."

"*Treasure Island?*" Russo asked.

"You can read?" Alicia gasped.

"Yes. Stevenson romanced the pirates of the old image and gave them an entirely new image."

"And the treasure maps?" Healey prompted.

"Well there's no dirty great X, which is a shame." Crouch smiled slightly. "But the script, or at least that which I can remember, should set us in the right direction. One thing Leno did tell me; the maps need to be read in order. Morgan wanted whoever followed, wife, children, whomever, to follow just one path."

"And we're to believe this great liar, this bandit and murderer, is telling the truth?" Russo wondered.

Crouch shrugged. "Maybe there is no treasure," he said. "But if that's the case, my friend, where did all his loot go?"

Russo struggled for an answer. Alicia told him to relax before he burst something then turned to Caitlyn. "You got anything else?"

"Well, Porto Bello is the real starting place."

"And where is that?"

"Panama," Caitlyn said as if everyone should know.

"Big place," Crouch prompted her.

"To put it into perspective, Porto Bello was the third main city in the New World at the time. And well-guarded. Morgan had balls, for sure. It's quite a story, the attack on the town, the trip upriver because of the shallow bay, but not for tonight."

Alicia flicked her eyes toward the window where a faint purplish smudge was beginning to show. "It's not tonight anymore." She sighed. "What a first day in the Caribbean."

"Didn't live up to your expectations?" Healey said with a grim smile.

"Well, I usually save the gun battles for the second week away."

"Anyway," Caitlyn said. "To show you the kind of man Morgan was—the governor of Panama sent a message asking how he'd overcome such a larger force of men and asked him not to attack Panama City. He also included a jewel with the note. Morgan sent him a pistol in return and said he'd be coming to reclaim it later. Now, more crucially, Morgan stayed in Porto Bello for over two months."

"Why is that crucial?" Healey asked quickly.

"Because, dopey, it gave him time. Time... to do anything. My guess is he wasn't drinking the whole time, though the man had a huge reputation as a drinker."

"You mean he had time to hide the bulk of his treasure?"

"Now you're talking. The take for this town alone was at least two hundred thousand pieces of eight, and that included the ransoming of prisoners. You see, these pirates or privateers, they were more ruthless than most of us know. Don't be taken in by Johnny Depp and co."

Alicia flicked at Healey's ear. "Beauty don't come with brains, eh kiddo? And Caitlyn, stop with the dissing of the Depp."

Crouch stepped forward. "All right, that's all well and good. But the maps are to be followed in a strict order. How do we know Porto Bello comes first?"

Caitlyn turned around in her seat. "How about the map?"

Crouch now showed them the work he'd been doing. "Well, take a look. This is all I can remember seeing, but it's not a bad start to a pirate treasure hunt, deadly as it may yet become."

He laid several sheets of paper out on the table.

## CHAPTER TWELVE

The team browsed through the various creations Crouch had made. Caitlyn sighed and then laughed a little as she handled the sheets of paper.

"Problem?" Crouch asked.

"I've seen better coastline drawings," Alicia said. "Just sayin'."

"Nothing wrong with them," Caitlyn said. "But I'm from the current age, Michael. All the maps I use are digital and can't be touched. I'm a researcher and might have started off picking through dusty shelves but the only dust I touch these days is on top of my computer. It feels odd, handling real paper research."

"I have to say," Russo spoke out, "that I don't see why we should follow them in order. Are you saying one may be a red herring? Or that they are deliberately jumbled?"

"Probably something to do with this." Alicia tapped the first map where Crouch had written several lines. "Follow these maps the right way, or you may have to bite the bullet."

Healey shook his head. "I don't get it."

"Basically, a warning," Caitlyn said. "Many of today's sayings were born in pirate days. Blood is thicker than water. Bitter end. Calm before the storm. And—bite the bullet." She pressed a few buttons. "Apparently sailors were given a bullet to bite on during difficult operations before the use of anesthetics. Hence, bite the bullet. Facing up to something rather unpleasant."

"You're not suggesting bloody traps?" Alicia moaned. "I hate traps. Healey—you're youngest. You go in first."

Caitlyn shrugged. "All we know is there *is* a warning. Don't you think we should heed it?"

Russo capitulated with a gesture. Alicia held up the map before her eyes. "Caitlyn, can you get a picture of the Panama coastline up on that screen?"

"Don't take that sketch as gospel," Crouch said. "My memory may be bordering on eidetic but it's not picture perfect by any means."

"Am I being stupid?" Healey asked, rather dangerously, as Caitlyn and Alicia compared the coastlines. "But why are we just assuming these are treasure maps? Because some diver said so? I mean, how lucky would it be to find these particular maps as they're searching all five wrecks?"

"You're suggesting they're fakes?" Crouch asked him. "Well, anything is possible. But don't be too cynical. Many chests have been brought up from the depths and they have some kind of radar that can identify objects. It's believed there could be thousands of bottles of rum on those ships. The *real* Captain Morgan rum. How cool is that?"

"So they aren't fakes?" Healey looked confused.

"My gut says not, my head says faint possibility. But I've been running with my gut for years."

"And in any case we'll soon find out," Alicia said. "This could very well be the right coastline."

"It could also be a hundred others." Russo peered over, playing devil's advocate.

"Just read the next sentence," Crouch said quietly.

"Uh?" Alicia looked over to the map's margin. "The Spaniards were between the devil and the deep blue sea, three forts down and we were in hot pursuit. That place was a rich picking and we used it as our port for as long as we pleased."

Crouch nodded. "I can't honestly recall the rest but the next paragraph I do remember talks about going 'inland with our blood money.'"

"And that leads us to this Porto Bello how?" Russo asked.

"The three forts," Caitlyn said immediately. "Morgan and his men destroyed them on the way into the town."

"So you knew all along?" Alicia clucked a little. "Why not tell us straight away?"

Crouch took a seat. "Because I prefer you question my reasoning, come at it a different way. If we all end up with the same answer then it has to be the right one. Besides, I only knew when Caitlyn described the battle for Porto Bello."

"I guess it could be possible that each site holds a further clue," Caitlyn added. "Or a portion of the loot.

"Only one way to find out," Crouch said, holding up a bottle of water in salute.

"Not exactly the drink I'd have chosen." Alicia placed the maps in a small pile. "But it'll do. Are we doing this then?"

"Oh yeah," Crouch said. "If only to catch Jensen and put that bastard out of business."

Caitlyn pulled a new website up on her computer. "Panama, here we come."

## CHAPTER THIRTEEN

Alicia soon realized that modern Porto Bello lacked a little of the majesty of old. Today an incredibly laid-back fishing village it was almost impossible to imagine it as the greatest Spanish port in the region. Peruvian gold, Spanish doubloons, unimagined riches from the Far East all came through this local capital, destined for Spain She knew that, despite all the attacks through the years, crumbled ruins of the old fortresses still stood among newer homes and dwellings, all adding an atmospheric ambiance to the little place. When the team arrived by boat, the residents took little notice of them.

People are always arriving by boat, their pilot told them. They don't linger long. Walk through the ruins and they're gone. Whatever they are looking for, they don't find it here.

Alicia led the way up the pebbly beach, knowing the others had her back and keeping a sharp eye open for Jensen and his cronies. No telling where they might pop up next. They had traveled over from Jamaica and they had come prepared. Alicia still hated boat travel, but fancied she should try to get used to it pretty soon since they were following a pirate around the Caribbean. Hours later though, she still hated it.

"Should've taken a plane," she muttered at Crouch.

"Too visible," he said. "We don't know where Jensen is and who he knows."

Alicia saw the logic, but hated the consequences. "Yeah, yeah."

Healey hitched his backpack a little tighter. Discreet boat travel also meant the team could bring weapons and other questionable equipment along with tents and sleeping bags, fodder, water, and much more. All of them wore heavy packs and sweated under the midday sun.

"Let's get out of this heat," Crouch said. "We're tourists. Let's tour."

With the blue waters at their backs and acres of greenery before them, the five found a rutted track and started to follow it. Crouch had a map of the area and produced it as they walked. Alicia wiped sweat from her brow and peered over.

"Where we headed?"

"Just trying to get our bearings. The old main port should be a few miles this way."

They trekked for a while, saying nothing. Healey and Russo ranged a little inland and watched the rear whilst Crouch and Alicia kept eyes open to the front. All they saw were a few local residents tending a few small fields or fishing offshore. Nobody looked up.

"Steady away," Alicia said. "Nobody in anyone's business. I think I could retire somewhere like this."

Crouch looked over. "Retire? Am I talking to the real Alicia Myles?"

"I don't mean tomorrow, for fuck's sake," she said, confirming that he was. "I mean . . . eventually."

"Still . . . you seem different than when last I saw you."

Alicia studied the glittering tops of the steady waves. "I'm trying, Michael. No more running into the sunset. No more moving away after every nasty little incident."

"You putting down roots?" He sounded a little disbelieving.

"Maybe. Let me put it this way—you've very lucky I came. Even more so than you thought." Of course she couldn't yet mention her other reason for coming. She needed privacy for that.

"Good." Crouch nodded. "Good. If there's anything I can do . . ."

"Oh, I'm sure there will be."

A long, green and furrowed track ran ahead until they could see the ruins of the old fort at the harbor. It wasn't much to look at now, but hundreds of years ago no doubt presented an imposing sight. The spectacle of tourists wandering around it now, their white hats pulled low and pink limbs turning even redder, doused even Crouch's enthusiasm for the hunt.

"So that's the harbor where Morgan eventually docked his ships?" Alicia shielded her eyes.

"Yep," Crouch said. "We're finally here. Let's see what it has to offer."

An uneventful hour passed as the team kicked around the ruins of the old fort and worked out some points of reference.

"One thing's for sure," Caitlyn said as she studied some nearby trees. "If Jensen's around we won't miss him."

Very few people passed as the team worked and the sun descended well past its zenith. Alicia spent some time studying the quiet, gleaming waters and tried to imagine what it must have been like to see several pirate ships anchored out there as their brethren scrambled to shore. Terror. Hatred. A sense of ruin. Invaders always left devastation in their wake.

Crouch called them all together and Alicia took the opportunity to eat. The maps appeared once more and Crouch drew their attention to the writing he'd memorized.

"Carried away it was, inland with our blood money. The channel behind, the forest ahead. We returned soon enough. Below decks among timber spars it was sent, but the trees they tell a story all their own. Our Black Book, buried there. As the crow flies, through two stands and at the foot of the hill."

"Clear as fucking mud that," Alicia said.

"It's not often we agree," Russo nodded, "but Milady has a point."

"The channel behind, the forest ahead." Crouch turned and

held up a hand. "Clearly marks the way. Of course, if these maps had never been found nobody would ever have known where to look."

"And the Black Book?"

"A reference to the treasure or the chests. Or whatever. Clearly they buried something out there and it needs to be found."

Crouch set off at a pace and the others hurried to catch up. Alicia saw that he almost looked hassled, as if doubting himself. Maybe he'd missed a line? It would be easy to do, despite a superb memory. She checked that the main channel into port was at her back and set off in as straight a line as she could manage. It occurred to her that, to the hard-drinking Morgan, a straight line might not be what it was to Michael Crouch, but she decided this wasn't the time to voice such thoughts. Maybe later.

The first stand of trees was dense and hard to push through, the second just up ahead after another stretch of flat ground. The heat shimmered all around and the sounds of insects filled the air. A bird swooped overhead, its bright plumage searing the skies with beauty. Alicia smelled earth, tree sap and mold, and walked upon a soft, loamy surface behind Russo, surprised that he held the branches back for her and wary in case he let one twang back. She would have. But maybe Russo was more of an adult.

Crouch entered the second stand of trees, still careful to check the position of the channel which they could now only see in glimmers through gaps between leaves and trees. The clearing here was a bit of a sunspot, radiating heat between walls of trees with a now darkening patch of sky up above. Crouch passed from sight.

Alicia pressed on, assessing the entire area as she went. They all had hands close to concealed weapons at this point since they knew Jensen could already be here. Crouch paused as a huge tree flummoxed him, its widespread branches and clinging leaves just too thick to penetrate.

"Stay there, Russo," he said. "I'll go around and pick you up on the other side."

"I'll join you." Alicia didn't want Crouch to venture off alone. She squeezed to his side and together they circumvented the big tree, resumed position and then waited for the others to come around.

"I am sorry about Beau."

Alicia blinked and felt a rush of surprise. Crouch had caught her out. "Oh, thanks. He got what was coming to him, I guess."

"I never pegged him for a traitor."

"Not even after he switched sides to join you?"

"No. I'm rarely a bad judge of character but I trusted that man."

Alicia hung her head. "Same here."

"I realize he used to be your boyfriend, Alicia, and I'm sorry."

"I made my own decision, Michael. The new one's much better."

It was supposed to ease the rising tensions, but Crouch didn't smile. "Matt Drake has many a demon to tame."

"Same as anyone who's lived past maturity."

The others were getting close now, but Crouch took one more moment to engage her. "I recruited Beau. He was my responsibility. Did I miss something? Or did I want to?"

Alicia could think of no quick reply, and then the rest of the team joined them. Crouch pushed ahead, threading the last of the trees and they found themselves in a sheltered clearing with a small brook running through the center.

"At the foot of the hill," Crouch intoned.

Beyond the burbling brook a sloping hill led directly up to another thick body of trees. Its banks were a verdant green and unsullied, the flowers that grew there wild and free. Crouch walked out toward the brook.

"So," he said, looking around. "Who's got the spade?"

Russo grunted. "Who'd ya think?" He shrugged out of his backpack and laid it on the floor.

"Does this feel right?" Alicia asked. "Does this really feel right to you?"

Crouch acquiesced with a slump of the shoulder. "Maybe, maybe not. But the verse *was* written on the set of maps and it led us here. What do we have to lose?"

"To be honest—" Alicia stared at the spade Russo produced from the backpack, a heavy, broad-bladed tool "—who wouldn't want to dig for buried treasure?"

"That's the spirit." Crouch found his own, smaller spade and made a beeline through the brook. "Take perimeter, Healey."

Alicia watched Healey leap off into the woods to start a recce and took in the general ambiance of the place. One might feel nothing bad had ever happened here. One might even feel nothing bad ever happened anywhere. But, sadly, these places were few and far between. Her friends, they all had their secrets. Healey had been mercilessly bullied by his brothers and shown no love by his parents and then run away to join the Army. He was still struggling. Russo continually controlled a Berserker rage, always coping and dealing with the knowledge that sometime, somewhere, it was going to erupt once more.

Her darker thoughts were interrupted by the sound of a shovel striking earth. Russo was already on the job. "Hey," she said. "I'd like to see a little of that action."

An hour passed, then two. The bright blue patch of canvas above their heads faded and shaded slowly to dark colors and then to pitch black. The team pitched tents and made them safe, then took a walk back toward the beach, leaving Healey and Caitlyn on guard. The air remained at a balmy temperature and the cool breeze felt good on their exposed skin. Nobody spoke a word during the short walk, but took in the relaxed atmosphere and almost utter quiet.

It was far from a common sensation they'd all enjoyed for most of their lives.

"Like I said before," Alicia eventually spoke up. "I could get used to this."

Russo started to nod in agreement and then appeared to remember who was speaking. "For once, I'd say your face is dirtier than your mind."

"Nothing wrong with a dirty mind, Robster."

A grunt. "Depends who you share it with."

Ahead now, the ruined fort overlooked the rolling waters and a bright moon shone upon rippling waves. All three soldiers drank it in for less than half a minute, and then Alicia voiced the thoughts of all three.

"Shit, let's get back to work. Any more of this I'm gonna lose my edge. Or go mad."

There was no more work that night, since the shadows filled all the spaces and flashlights weren't good enough to work by. The holes were already deep but nothing that glittered had revealed itself so far. The team took a few hours' rest, switched for sentry duty and were up before dawn the next day. A quick meal and they were back at it. Caitlyn fetched water from the clear stream and left it for the diggers to cool themselves off. Russo was already stripped to the waist by early morning, making Alicia shade her eyes every time she glanced over in his direction.

"Jeez, man, it's like staring at a pint of milk."

"And you should cover up," Caitlyn added. "Sunburn ain't choosy."

"Shit, I feel like I've inherited a couple of bossy sisters."

Alicia then put down her spade and climbed out of the earthy hole she'd been digging. She took a long look at their day's work and met Crouch's already knowing eyes.

"It ain't here, boss."

Crouch climbed up and sat on the edge of his own small void in the earth. "I just don't get it. Did I miss something?"

"Hey, can't win 'em all. If every treasure hunt was a success it wouldn't be worth searching for."

Caitlyn brought them all water. "Why not check the maps again?"

Crouch studied his mud-caked fingers. "First, a wash I think."

"You and me both," Alicia murmured, then flicked her head up. "But not together!"

They wandered down the free-flowing brook. Crouch stopped first around a slight bend, courteously letting her stroll further away to find some privacy. When Alicia came across a suitable place, she knelt in the stream and took her time washing. It was a perfunctory cleansing; she was at heart a soldier and would never let herself become too vulnerable in such an open place. She made do with what she had, and that was good enough.

As they returned to camp, Russo suddenly gave out a yell. "Oh, hell!"

Alicia sprang into action, racing over to the big man and signaling Healey to take a closer look at the perimeter.

"What is it?"

"I don't know. But it sure as hell ain't treasure."

Of course, Russo did know. He was waiting for Alicia and Crouch to come over before indicating his find. Caitlyn came up as they stared in silence.

"Bones," Alicia said, and felt a little shiver despite the increasing warmth of the day.

"Old bones," Caitlyn said. "This might actually make sense."

"Why? How can you tell?"

"Well, obviously I can't tell the exact date they were placed here but looking at the condition I'd have to say a considerable time ago. And they were buried. And see the strongbox underneath? Somebody's going to have to grab that."

Russo didn't hesitate, but carefully and respectfully placed the bones aside and hefted the strongbox. It was a basic, metal container with a rudimentary lock, also clearly many years old. He brought it out of the hole and placed it on the ground.

"Wait," Crouch said as the soldier gripped the lid. "Caitlyn? What did you mean when you said this makes sense?"

"I did a bit of digging of my own," Caitlyn said with a smile. "The part about the Black Book bugged me. Why include it? Why talk about burying it? Surely it had to have some significance to Morgan and his treasures."

"And what is a black book?" Crouch asked.

Alicia reached down to help Russo back out of the hole as Caitlyn spoke.

"It started as far back as the 1300s and was a listing of maritime laws and codes of conduct. Offenders were always punished hard. To the pirates it was a collection, physical or verbal, of those of their own kin that committed crimes against them. Their 'black book' was buried here."

"You couldn't have mentioned that before we started digging?" Alicia asked.

"Well, I wasn't sure. And you all seemed so eager."

"And now we know." Crouch nodded at Russo, who tore the worn metal apart with his bare hands. The edges were sharp and ragged, and Russo took his time. Inside, they found a sheaf of old parchment, partly covered in a thick, black script. Crouch stared at it hard but didn't dare touch it.

"We can't mess with this," he said. "The experts should be allowed to figure it out. But I'll say one thing for sure—there's no treasure here."

"The map was an account of Morgan burying the transgressors," Caitlyn said. "Maybe we should move on to the next one."

"Not exactly," Crouch said. "There was more."

He moved away and dug out the maps once more. Alicia walked with him. Healey popped his head around a tree to report the all clear and then vanished once more. Still, they were undisturbed.

"Carried away it was, inland with our blood money. The channel behind, the forest ahead. We returned soon enough. Below decks among timber spars it was sent, but the trees they tell a story all their own. Our Black Book, buried there. As the crow flies, through two stands and at the foot of the hill."

"Now it makes sense," Alicia said with a grin.

"Always does when you know the answer," Crouch said off-handedly. He was concentrating on the map. "Come with me. All of you."

The team gathered as quickly as they could, Russo still slapping at his trousers to remove clinging mud and shrugging into a T-shirt. Backpacks were hefted and Caitlyn pointed out the precariousness of their find.

"Don't worry. We'll report it as soon as we can. Problem is, we're backed into a corner here with nowhere to go."

"You could always ask a few contacts to find Jensen," Alicia suggested. "Cut out the treasure hunt."

Crouch looked at her as if she might be mad. "You're kidding me, right? That's why we're *here*."

Alicia sighed. She knew his love of treasure hunting came from a rich youth reading old books and getting into trouble. She also knew he'd dreamed of a job like this through decades of army duties. The joy, for Crouch, was the hunt itself.

Their boss took them back toward the old fort and the waters beyond. Alicia picked out several yachts bobbing on the surface, their polished hulls and golden ornaments shining under a rising sun, their white sails billowing. Closer still, half a dozen tourists walked the ruins of the old castle, cameras dangling around their necks.

Crouch stared at the harbor.

"Imagine it. Half a dozen pirate ships at anchor, day and night for two months. Stocked full with provisions, goods to barter and pirate plunder. Untold wealth. Surrounded by it every moment, it would make a man become suspicious. On edge. It could make a man so distrustful he might come up with a crazy, brilliant plan."

"What plan?" Russo asked.

"Scupper a ship. Let it go down, the treasure with it."

Alicia frowned. "How? What? I mean . . . how would they ever retrieve it?"

"It's a shallow bay. Remember what Caitlyn said? Morgan and his men had to sail upriver by boat to take out the forts. They would have sailed the ships in very carefully a bit later."

"Wouldn't people have noticed a sinking ship?" Caitlyn asked.

"Undoubtedly. But who would question it? Most of the locals probably welcomed the sight of it. Invent some kind of story. Mutiny. Drunken men. Whatever. And let it all die down. There's even the possibility that the men Morgan buried with the Black Book were thieves, trying to steal some of the treasure, which drove him to come up with this audacious plan."

"All right. But what's your evidence?" Caitlyn asked.

"The map. The script. Below decks on timber spars it was sent."

Alicia shook her head. "That's pretty vague, boss."

"Of course it is. It's meant to be vague. A pirate isn't about to make it easy for you. But *timber spars* are how a ship ends up on the bottom of the sea when it's scuppered and the word *sent*—I believe means exactly what it says."

Alicia turned her face toward the bay. "So it's out there? Somewhere."

"I believe so. Maybe a spot of research would confirm the number of ships, though I doubt we'd get lucky enough to see their positions. In any case they'd be as close to shore as possible. Pirates weren't known for putting in extra work."

"So how do we find out?"

Crouch indicated an area in the distance where rows of huts and makeshift shopfronts had been erected on the beach. "We rent diving gear."

## CHAPTER FOURTEEN

In the spirit of diving for treasure the sea bottom gave up very little. Alicia remembered some figure about there being over a million shipwrecks on the sea floor, with 70 percent of them not found. In three recent finds alone estimators guessed they'd netted $4.5 billion in loot. Somebody once said, "We know more about the surface of the moon than the bottom of the sea. It's the last frontier."

One estimate put the figure of sunken loot at $60 billion.

Small wonder then, that thousands of people and mega-rich companies put time and effort into combing the waves for them. She might even do it herself if she had known what the hell she was actually doing. But this diving shit?

She had a bad track record for underwater exploration. Her last had resulted in a subsurface explosion that took out a potential lost kingdom. No biggie. This time, she donned the mask and strapped on the air tanks with some trepidation and sank below the waves in no hurry at all. The team had spent hours in fruitless research, then decided to take their best guesses and start exploring. All except Caitlyn, who hadn't yet learned how to dive. The proprietor that rented them their diving gear wasn't much help, except to tell them his trade wasn't exactly booming.

In short, they dived for long hours, then dived some more. They didn't take enough breaks. They became tetchy, anxious. Where on earth was Jensen? Perhaps he'd already known that the town of Porto Bello was a red herring.

They slept that night again in tents, and were back on the

beach before the proprietor. He wasn't surprised to see them, since they'd already booked the night before and handed over a fat tip. The man didn't say much, face creased by sun, winds and saltwater, but the look in his eyes told them he knew they were far from curious tourists.

Under the waves was a dark, gloomy world, pleasant near the surface but descending into murk the further they swam offshore. Crouch led the way, taking them to where calculations showed the closest possible anchor point was for Morgan's ships. From there they fanned out.

And became lost.

In the end, the team could do no more. They enlisted the help of two local divers that earned their living from diving and teaching others how to. Truth be told, they were more laid-back than a deck chair, but once properly motivated they worked like men possessed. It still took the rest of the day but by sunset one of the men had located something which he described to the team as *timber spars.*

The words electrified Crouch, Alicia could see. It was all they could do to pass another night wondering, talking around a beach campfire, and then start back at first light. The divers did all the work, and presently two more came to help. Pretty soon, a bevy of relaxed locals were setting up on the beach, jobs ignored for the day, rum punch and smoothies being poured and speculations made. With the local dive team swelled to six, Crouch and Russo were the only ones now out there, trying to help.

They found the strongbox that afternoon and hauled it back to the beach. Crouch took charge but invited all the locals to watch and bear witness to whatever they found.

Crouch held a hand out. "I think we need a tool this time. A chunky screwdriver maybe?"

Alicia rummaged in her pack and muttered, "Pretty sure you used a tool last time."

Russo was out of earshot. Healey stood with Caitlyn, the latter resting her head on the former's shoulders and smiling lightly. Alicia didn't have the heart to comment as Crouch poked at the strongbox.

"Found a weak spot," he muttered. "Just have to . . . there we are."

The box was a little bigger than the last, sturdy and coated with silt and even a barnacle or two. Crouch pried it open with a little help and then stared at its contents. To a person, the assembled throng leaned forward.

"No doubloons," Caitlyn said with disappointment.

"But there is something," Crouch said.

He reached inside and drew forth several golden necklaces, bracelets and a pile of small trinkets. As he rummaged through, a trinket box was revealed, tacked together with dark wood and with a sliding front drawer and lid that revealed several fine drawings of ladies and gentlemen when raised. There was a small mirror, ruined through time, and a smaller box inside. Crouch immediately pointed to the date inscribed into the underside of the lid.

"Oh, dear God. We may not have found the treasure, but this, to some people, could be just as important."

Alicia understood, of course. The date was 1665. This trinket box would have been present in Porto Bello at the same time that Captain Henry Morgan sacked it.

"These are the people's treasures," Crouch continued. "Sentimentals. Personal possessions. Morgan didn't want them but couldn't bring himself to give them back."

"So he sank them to the bottom of the sea?" Healey asked with disbelief.

"I guess pirates do that," Caitlyn said.

"And left a map to their whereabouts?" Healey still sounded unsure.

"Could be a touch of guilt. A touch of mischief. He knew they'd never be found without the maps, which he carried away. One thing has occurred to me now, though, on making these two finds—maybe the maps were Morgan's way of making a log. Cataloguing timelines and events. It would make sense."

The locals were crowding close now, trying to get a feel for what was inside the box. Crouch asked one of the divers to find a phone and call somebody in authority. Alicia fancied someone had just mightily increased their workload.

"This is a good find," she said. "It may even give some people closure. Heirlooms and valuables like this are all family treasures and close to somebody's heart. If only they can match them with the right people."

"I'm sure they will try," Crouch said and rose. "But we're not done here, guys. As you can see, this isn't what we're looking for."

"Nothing like," Healey said.

"So what's next?" Alicia asked.

"Next? We visit a treasure island."

## CHAPTER FIFTEEN

Feeling rested and uplifted, the team soon found themselves on a flight to Haiti. Crouch decided they had lost too much time with the frustrating and yet satisfying search of Porto Bello and needed to catch up. They did manage to rent a private plane though, which helped with the contents of their backpacks. Private airfields and planes were more plentiful here than palm trees.

Healey sat beside Caitlyn, the two talking quietly, whilst Crouch spread out along the back seat, taking the time to rest. Alicia found herself dozing alongside Russo whilst fielding calls from her primary team and her boyfriend, Drake.

"Can't do without me," she said cheerily.

Russo looked across. "Desperate men need desperate things."

"What the hell's that supposed to mean? And stop with the pretend complaining, Russo. I know you love me."

The big soldier choked.

"Well, we do work well together. As a team."

A sigh. "Y'know, I guess we do."

"So, ease up on the criticism, eh? Tell me, how are you really doing?"

Beneath the many thick layers Russo was a complex man, always trying to control the rage and make himself a better person. If one thing could be said about him, night and day, it was that he never stopped trying.

"The struggle continues," he said simply.

"You think you'll get used to it?"

"I don't think this is something a person could ever get used to. That could be referred to as sweeping the problem under the carpet. With me, it's always here." He tapped his forehead. "Always recognized and kept in check."

Alicia leaned back in her seat. "That's a hell of a way to live, Russo. A hell of a way."

The big soldier shrugged. "It is what it is. What about you?" He eyed her. "Am I detecting something different?"

"Are you?"

"Well, you seriously asked about my wellbeing. The old Alicia would have rather eaten a moose's hoof."

Alicia smiled. "I hear they're pretty tasty. We're soldiers, Russo. We don't feel. We don't talk about feelings. We get down to the job."

"Nothing else?"

"There's the possibility of something else. I don't know what. But all my life I've been running. Running from home and then from enemies and then from one damn battle to the next. I've changed all that now."

Russo settled back. "Really? How?"

"Easy. I stopped bloody running. You have to face what comes. That's what makes us the people we are."

"For good or bad." He appeared to agree.

"Struggle gives you strength. It makes the next battle a little easier."

"Jeez, woman, that's a pretty dour outlook."

Alicia punched him on the arm. "It's my new slogan."

They both laughed, perfectly aware of the maxim Alicia had always lived by. *One life, live it.* An ideal like that worked with any scenario.

The pilot announced they were a half hour away from their destination and that brought Crouch awake, shaking his head and asking for coffee. Caitlyn soon joined them along with

Healey and they began to discuss the next stage. Crouch unrolled the second map and laid it out before them.

"Henry Morgan's special place. His sanctuary. An island off Haiti called Île-à-Vache, also Isla Vaca. It was here that he felt safe and planned assaults on settlements such as Cartagena, where much of the gold the Spanish brought from Peru was held in transit. Of course, it was also the site of many accidents and deaths since it was where the pirates . . . um, shall we say 'let their hair down.'"

Caitlyn had also looked into Morgan's antics. "Ah, this was the place where Morgan's flagship, the *Oxford*, sent by England to protect Port Royal and then gifted to Morgan *by* Port Royal, was utterly destroyed. Drunken sailors accidentally ignited the ship's explosive cache, killing many and making deserters of many more. An event like that was seen as a bad omen. But Isla Vaca itself is considered one of the most beautiful of all the Caribbean islands, with some of the best scenery. And, naturally, many shipwrecks surround its rocky, reef-lined coastline."

"No diving for me," Alicia put in. "Ever again."

"Well, they do seem to have a confused image of Morgan around here," Crouch said. "The current tourist port of Isla Vaca is named after him."

"Romancing the pirates," Alicia said. "Helps with the cash flow."

"Y'know," Russo said to her as the plane banked, "I can imagine you as a pirate. Lady Alicia and Calico Jack, plunderers of the high seas."

"Fuck off, Russo."

"An interesting and more pertinent fact to our mission," Crouch then took it up, "is that in 2004 a team of researchers found another of Morgan's vessels only four meters below the surface of the sea."

"Like I said—" Alicia coughed "—no diving."

"That's hardly diving," Healey pointed out.

"Well, it just shows how close these shipwrecks are. Anchored at shore, accidental damage. Some still unsalvaged."

"And where to now?" Russo asked. "We can hardly start digging in Port Morgan."

Crouch rustled the map. "We're heading for the other side of the island. It's pretty unclear, if I'm honest, but that, my friends, it the reason we chartered a seaplane."

"Really?" Alicia raised both brows.

"Well, one of the reasons."

"Ten minutes out," the pilot informed them.

"Speaking of seaplanes and chartering," Caitlyn said. "One day we will have to meet Mr. Sadler, our mysterious benefactor."

Crouch nodded. "Oh, he's not so mysterious. Rolland funds all kinds of searches and treks. At heart, he's a kid, a treasure hunter like me. Just so happens he's also a multi-millionaire."

The team prepped their packs, always ready for anything. Crouch rolled up the map after explaining why they were headed for what looked like a deserted beach.

"It's singled out in the only piece of script I could remember," he admitted. "If this comes up blank, we could be all washed up."

"On to map three?" Healey suggested.

"Well, there's always that. But it would be good to get something solid behind us. Something real. Treasure-wise," he added with a grin.

"Always the treasure." Caitlyn laughed.

"On my mind when I wake up, on my mind when I fall asleep."

"It amazes me how many ships they find, how many they salvage and search, and yet so little treasure," Healey said. "I have to say—"

"Whoa," Alicia interrupted. "Is this our deserted bay?"

The plane had been banking quite a bit as the pilot followed Crouch's directions, flying over hills and valleys and the bluest of sparkling streams. Sunlight was the golden treasure here, and it bathed the whole beautiful land with its bright bounty. As they stared out of the window a canopy of trees ended and an arc of gilded beach began, lapped by a glittering sea. If that was all they could see, it would be a soothing vision, but Alicia had spotted something quite the opposite.

Seaplanes.

"They're anchored just offshore," she said. "Three of them."

"Anchored?" Russo said. "Isn't that like talking about an elephant's hoof?"

"Whatever." Alicia didn't turn away from the window. "And what is it with you and hoofs anyway?"

"Do you see any men?" Healey was yet to make it to the window.

Alicia studied the scene below. Three white seaplanes bobbed a hundred feet away from the beach. Men sat in the floats and one sat with his legs dangling out of an open door. Two more men piloted a dinghy and, as their plane drew closer and the beach opened up, a whole bunch of figures could be seen congregated near the tree line. Tents were arrayed all around as well as a larger canopy.

"Looks like these guys have been here a while," Alicia said. "Made themselves right at home."

Some were stripped to the waist, others wore T-shirts and shorts, but most were at work, digging holes in the ground. Alicia imagined they almost certainly had a perimeter in place to ward off nosey neighbors and that the perimeter guards would be on the two-way right about now.

"Fly away," she said. "Just bank clear. We can come in from the south and through the tree cover."

Instantly, the plane banked hard, making Crouch stumble. Luckily he landed in one of the seats with nothing more than a look of embarrassment. The seaplane flew up and away, but already the men on the beach were staring at them, pointing, and arms were gesticulating back and forth.

"They recognized us. Shit," Alicia grunted.

"How could they?" Caitlyn showed her naivety.

"Binos," Healey said. "The perimeter team would have them, not to mention a few spotters on the beach."

As the pilot climbed higher, Alicia saw one of the pilots scrambling into his seaplane, quickly followed by a half dozen armed men.

"Better break out your guns, boys," she said. "It's time to earn our keep."

## CHAPTER SIXTEEN

This particular model of seaplane had front and rear doors, and two long pontoons to land on. Crouch saw no profit in staying too high so the pilot brought the craft lower, trying not to complain but staring at the approaching enemy with eyes wide with fear.

"Don't worry, Iceman," Alicia said. "We'll sort this in a jiffy."

She hefted her rifle. Russo loaded his own beside her and Healey took the other side of the plane. As the other plane approached, Crouch cried: "Bank left and down!"

A jerk of the controls and a lightening of the stomach, and Alicia saw their plane dive under the other. She held onto the door handle as the plane came back up, but their enemy banked too, diving again. Caitlyn fell to the floor. Crouch held onto a seatbelt, refusing to strap in, in case he was needed. Their pilot came around in a wide loop and suddenly the planes were broadside to each other.

"I've seen this before," Alicia said as she opened the door. "But it was between galleons, not planes."

She poked the rifle out, steadied, and opened fire. Bullets slammed across airspace and into the other plane, shredding the metal skin. The pilot veered away. Alicia saw men falling in all directions.

"Modern age, modern warfare," Russo said in answer to her comment. "At least we can't sink."

"Well, eventually we could but we'd have to crash-land first."

Crouch tried to direct their pilot who seemed to be frozen at the controls. He climbed out of his seat to ask if he could take charge of the plane. The pilot stared at him aghast.

"You kidding?"

"No, sir. I am an accomplished military pilot."

"Where was your last flight and what happened?"

"Um, well, over Niagara Falls in a helicopter and we ... won."

"You *won?* What do you mean?"

"It was a gun battle," Crouch admitted with a sigh.

"Dude, you should stay away from things that fly."

Alicia held on with grim determination. Their pilot was flying straight at the other plane, but then swung right at an order from Crouch. As the two winged crafts passed, Healey opened fire from his side of the plane. At the same time bullets ripped into their own hull. The sound of tortured metal and the terrible thudding of bullets filled the small space for seconds that felt like hours. The team hit the floor; the pilot shrieked.

"We're getting the hell outta here!" he cried out.

"No," Crouch told him. "Show your tail to them and they'll quickly shoot you out of the skies. We have to stay fully mobile and as cunning as possible."

The pilot girded his loins. Alicia held firm to the door, and Healey followed suit. Russo eyed it all as if wanting to push her out of the way and get involved. Their plane descended, then rose sharply, leveling off alongside the other.

More bullets were traded. Alicia picked out a man this time and took him down, seeing his falling body push aside two more. As the other plane passed she saw a big mercenary crowding his way through and out the door, jumping down to the pontoon with incredible confidence.

Or incredible stupidity.

She preferred to think the latter, but didn't think too hard. As the planes came around again, she lined him up.

"Oh, holy crap."

Concentrating on the man and not his ammo she'd failed to spot the H&K machine gun.

"Dive! Dive!" she cried, feeling like a submarine pilot. "Fucking dive!"

The pilot reacted instantly, hearing the urgency in her voice. Bullets grated across the top of their craft and lumps of shredded metal rained down. The pilot cleverly came back up the other side and lined Alicia up for a bit of retaliation.

She was ready. Steadying both aim and balance she destroyed glass and metal and even the struts of wings. Her own plane then plunged and her stomach hit the roof of her mouth.

"Wha...?"

"Have to drop her down a bit." The pilot grimaced. "The altitude's stressing her out."

Alicia figured it might be the pilot not the plane, but got on with it. Russo stared at her with demanding eyes.

"Go on, Robster. You can have a go."

As the enemy plane came lower too, descending on top of them, Alicia saw the beach flying upwards. Most of the men had climbed out of the hole and were heading toward jeeps, the tents and their contents forgotten. Some carried guns, but others just ran. She wondered if many of them were just hired help. The two remaining seaplanes still bobbed in place, though several dinghies now surrounded them, filled with men.

An idea came to her, crazy but workable, and that was enough.

"Take us down to the sea," she said. "And don't hang around. If they see this coming, we're sunk."

Russo laughed. "Sunk?"

"Literally."

The pilot, to his credit, didn't question her, just headed toward the glittering waters with the other plane left wondering above. Alicia began to see faces more clearly, and get a grasp for the weapons they faced.

"Mostly handguns," she said. "If this is Jensen's crew they're cheaply outfitted and running on air. No wonder he wants a score so bad."

"Could be his last gasp. Crew losing patience. At each other's throats. That kind of thing," Healey said.

"Ready to mutiny?" Caitlyn asked with a scamp's grin.

"Jensen figures he's a pirate captain." Alicia shook her head. "Maybe he'll end up like one."

By now the plane was approaching the blue waters of Haiti and most of the men aboard the dinghies had turned to watch. Some readied weapons. Others sat without moving as if wanting none of the violence.

"Ready for this?" Alicia asked.

"For what?" Russo asked. "What's the plan?"

"We take another plane."

The pontoons skimmed across and then plowed through the water, arrowing straight for the leading enemy plane. It slowed rapidly, forcing the Gold Team to hang on tightly, and the pilot sent it in a little swerve toward the end.

The craft came alongside nicely.

Alicia flung open the side door and followed Healey out into the bright, hot day. With weapons screaming they were all shock and awe, fire and brimstone. They jumped down to the pontoon and spread out. A dinghy was shot to pieces, its men sent sprawling or tumbling overboard. Two lay bleeding, their own weapons cast aside. Men swam hard for the shore. Alicia concentrated on the second dinghy. Their enemies, though, were no slouches and were already bringing their own weapons to bear.

Healey came out of the same side door just as a bullet struck the frame around it. He ducked quickly, swearing. Alicia shot the man that held the gun, and saw him topple backwards. But they were exposed now. It was time to act.

The planes had drifted closer. Without missing a beat, she leapt to the prow of the shattered dinghy, used it for balance and momentum, and sprang onto the pontoon of the enemy seaplane. A man met her, striking out with a knife. She hurled her body to the side, using the hull of the plane to stop her fall and bounce back up. Her right fist connected hard with his jaw, her left with a set of ribs and then the barrel of her gun with his right temple. He collapsed, unmoving.

Healey came next, outpacing and probably out-gracing Russo when it came to nimble movement. Two more mercs stood on the pontoon, and were both targeting Alicia. Healey fired at one and kicked at the other, unbalancing both, sending them slithering between the pontoon and the body of the plane. Both gone, but not necessarily neutralized.

Alicia gripped the door of the plane and pulled.

Behind her, Russo was concentrating on the second dinghy. Beyond that battle the beach was becoming more and more deserted as mercs drove off in jeeps, all running as if someone had lit a fire at their heels. Alicia wondered if Jensen had sacrificed the planes and the men around them. A decoy. Nothing would surprise her.

But a second seaplane certainly wouldn't hurt.

Inside the cabin the pilot and two mercs remained. A bullet clanged off the framework at her side. She wasted no time returning fire. She shot the mercs and then stared hard at the pilot.

"You know what to do."

Without a word he flung open the door and leapt out of the plane. Alicia scrambled into the cockpit and took a look out the panoramic windows. Their own seaplane bobbed even closer now, protected by Crouch and largely untroubled now save for the sudden appearance of the original mercenary plane. Alicia spun and shouted a warning to Russo who switched his attentions from a rebellious merc to the swooping plane. He lifted his aim and opened fire, raking its side as men leaned out to draw a bead on the resting seaplane. Crouch also fired through an open door. Two men slithered out, falling into the sea. The rest jumped back inside as the pilot banked hard.

Alicia waved across the water at Crouch's pilot. "Fire her up!"

Jensen's last seaplane, the fourth, was also winding her engines up now and Alicia motioned Healey inside and then to the controls.

"Not sure about this crazy idea!" he cried.

"Two are better than one," she answered back.

Healey jumped inside and slammed the door at his back. The water around them was scattered with struggling and dead mercs, all heading for the fourth plane, a surviving dinghy, or even to shore. One of the dinghies floated in a heap, riddled with bullets.

"Jensen's not even here," Russo was saying. "They're fleeing and it's now a rout."

"He got what he came for," Alicia said, "and decided not to hang around."

"Man's a pirate all right. Through and through."

Alicia shook her head slightly, watching Healey and the other pilot through the glass of the cockpit. The man looked like he was ready to take off. Their other plane was taxiing through the waves, faster and faster. Healey goosed the throttle and shot forward. Plumes and showers of water arced through the air. Alicia strapped in as Healey poured on the speed and then took off right behind their other seaplane with Crouch and Caitlyn aboard. As soon as they were level the soldiers unbuckled and readied their weapons. Both enemy seaplanes were out of sight for the moment, but Alicia expected them to return.

Unless they decided to run.

*Doubtful*, she thought. The battle had been hard-fought so far.

They banked and came around, their vision suddenly filled with an approaching plane. Healey dove fast and Alicia lost her balance, falling to one knee. The eyebrow she arched toward Healey said it all.

Healey grimaced. "Saved your life."

"Just check the rearview mirror next time, eh?"

They came around, and Alicia caught a momentary glimpse of all four seaplanes leaning through the air, making wide turns and attempting to hold onto their bearings. As the planes leveled out, rifles and handguns popped out of windows and some of the more adventurous men opened doors and slithered onto the pontoons. Alicia shook her head at the two that weren't anchored inside.

"Death wish."

Healey took a target and came alongside. Alicia zeroed in on the pilot, but the buffeting winds and shifting metal hull sent her shot wide. Still, other targets were hit as the two planes blasted past each other. Russo, alongside her, winced to see a man fall and end up dangling from his harness beneath the plane.

"Poor bastard."

Alicia said nothing, but tended to agree. They might be enemies, these men, but nobody wanted to see them suffer. She watched Crouch's plane scream alongside the other enemy craft, propellers whining, engines screaming, and saw windows blown out on either side. All four planes descended toward the rippling waters as if wary of the next pass and adding odds to their chances of survival.

Alicia steadied her aim with the window frame, wedged her body into the small space as best she could, and breathed easily. The peril, the skies, the entire Caribbean faded away until it was the gun barrel and her target. She fired hard as the other plane approached, bullets raking the cockpit and sending the pilot slamming back into his seat.

Instantly, the seaplane veered toward them, the pontoons growing bigger, men at the windows increasing in size. Healey jerked the controls violently, gaining space. The tip of a wing slammed past the bottom of their hull, shredding metal like paper, and then fell away, the enemy plane falling like a rock. Healey's eyes were wide.

"Ah, shit, that's bad."

Alicia turned on him. "How bad?"

"We're definitely gonna crash, I just don't know how bad."

"Bollocks."

Alicia watched Crouch and the other pilot engaged in an aerial dogfight, bullets strafing the skies. Loud pings and the wrench of metal could be heard even over the plane noise. The seaplane they'd shot down hit the waves at that moment, even as Healey struggled, bits of white wing and nosecone, propeller and rear wing shredding and grinding away. The craft somersaulted and then started to sink slowly; several pairs of arms and shoulders visibly swimming away.

"Hey, that's encouraging." Russo squinted down.

"Not for us, dumbass," Alicia grated. "They're daft enough to sit down there and wait for us."

Russo shrugged. "I think, by now, they'll all have figured out Jensen left them behind."

"Let's hope."

"Shut up," Healey said then. "And strap in. We're doing this right now."

As Alicia scrambled to find a seat the young soldier lost a good chunk of altitude, sending her stomach soaring. The blue expanse of the sea appeared in all their horizons as Healey leveled off.

He turned them toward the beach.

"What if you overshoot?" Russo grumbled.

"Then we'll be deader than we would be if we hit the waves wrong."

"Your friggin' pilot manner needs some work, kid."

Healey hauled back on the controls, leveled out the pontoons and cut the engine. The floats hit the relatively flat water hard, skipped, then came down again. Alicia felt like she was fighting her seatbelt, jerked back and forth, ribs bruised and chafed where the material ground against her. The plane skipped again, losing a lot of momentum, and then ran up the beach, furrowing in hard. The final jounce shook every bone in her body and made her teeth rattle, but the craft came to a sudden stop and they were all still alive.

Unbuckling and leaning forward, she clapped Healey hard on the shoulder. "Well done, Zack."

"No worries."

Immediately shrugging off the landing and the tension, the soldiers acted fast, focusing on the next potential events where mercs might even now come after them. Alicia flung open the doors of the plane and leapt down, gun up. Russo followed suit on the other side and Healey scrambled after them.

The beach was empty, the waters clear. No mercs lay in wait for them.

Alicia looked to the skies. "Oh fuck, here comes Crouch."

## CHAPTER SEVENTEEN

Alicia almost ducked as the seaplane carrying Crouch and Caitlyn zoomed overhead and whipped the tops of trees as it rose, closely followed by the second merc craft. Alicia was quick to raise her gun and fire up into the dirty metal underside, ripping several holes as it passed by. Russo was a second slower but just as effective.

Healey flexed his fingers, shrugged his shoulders and looked for his gun.

"C'mon, Healey," Alicia growled. "Get your bloody act together."

The wry glare showed just how shook up he was.

Above, Crouch's seaplane looped around and once more skimmed the trees. Alicia saw the pilot's face and then the sudden angle of descent.

"Oh hell, he's landing."

"They'll be sitting ducks!" Healey cried.

"They know that. Something must be damaged." Alicia quickly cast around for an answer, saw an intact dinghy and raced for it. "Keep on hounding the mercs' plane!"

She raced off, but at that moment the mercs' plane itself roared overhead, and made Alicia almost pull up. The angle of descent was beyond harsh, the beach itself was beckoning. She reasoned that at least one of their bullets must have caused a great deal of damage. Smoke billowed from the engine.

A man jumped, landing hard in the shallows, and lay unmoving as Alicia watched. The plane then nose-dived into the beach, huge shards of it breaking off and catapulting toward the sea where it would sink and lie and eventually merge with all the old shipwrecks. More men claimed by the depths. An explosion and a fireball sent her diving to the ground. The groan of wreckage and not survivors told her the cost of the crash.

Unable to stop, she rose fast and looked out to sea. Crouch's plane still flew, the angle much better now, the craft steady. It bobbed down and then turned and taxied around. Alicia tried to push the burning seaplane from her mind and hurried over to the dinghy.

Her mind had already turned toward Crouch and Caitlyn and the pilot; she prayed they were unhurt.

In the aftermath, the Gold Team knew there could be no rest, no reflection. Jensen was already headed elsewhere and no one knew what he'd found. Though they were all safe they were battered and bruised. The drifting pall of smoke from the still-burning wreckage would attract attention.

And they still had work to do right here, right now.

On gaining the beach, a sore-looking Crouch loped immediately up its slight slope toward the tree line. Alicia looked over at Russo and Healey, who were ensuring no stragglers remained and forming a perimeter. Russo gave her a thumbs up.

Alicia followed Crouch as he closed in on three wide holes that Jensen's men had dug.

"The placement works in conjunction with the maps," he said. "We didn't have the script, he did. That shouldn't happen again, not completely."

"No way of telling what he found," Caitlyn said. "But he left a few things behind."

"Cleared out in a hurry," Alicia said. "Could be good or bad for us, but I'm guessing at the latter."

"Pessimist." Caitlyn reached the edge of the first hole and peered inside.

"Comes with the job."

Alicia stared down into the muddy cavity. Tree branches and a large stump weaved a tangled web on the far side. Closer and deeper the hole stood empty, echoing like a lost dream. Crouch was already on to the second and Alicia followed. Caitlyn lingered to make sure their inspection was a thorough one.

The second pit yielded the best find of the three. An open strongbox lay at the bottom and, although it had been rifled, still held several sheets of parchment and an old brooch. Half a dozen objects lay embedded in the dirt and sand, and one sheet had been crumpled up.

Crouch shook his head. "Not a single ounce of respect."

"At this level of pay," Alicia said. "Plant-life competes with them."

"So let's see what we've got."

Crouch jumped into the hole and picked up the strongbox. "Well, it's the same era as the last, same kind of design. Certainly possible it came from around here and from similar circumstances. No clue as to what else might have been inside."

Caitlyn came over. "And the parchments?"

"Centuries old, but nothing pertinent to us. More work for the historians, I guess. You can take a look, Caitlyn, in case your eyes spot something mine don't."

"Sure." She scrambled down to his side.

Alicia stretched and eyed the last hole. Like the first it was empty, with no clues as to what might have been there. Maybe nothing. There were no impressions within the cavity to lead her to think something had once rested there.

Crouch scrambled up top. "We shouldn't linger. I think it is time to move." He turned to the pilot. "Is the plane sea- and airworthy, my friend?"

"It will be fine so long as I don't have to explain the bullet holes."

"Where we're headed, that won't be an issue."

"Not sure I like the sound of that."

"You could always sit it out. You don't have to come along."

"You gonna buy me a new plane, right?"

Crouch hesitated. "I wouldn't say *new.* Like for like, maybe."

"And if you guys find Morgan's haul?"

"Maybe you'll get two. One for the weekends."

"All right." The pilot watched Alicia. "You take it. I'll wait on Jamaica."

The team gathered and made their way out of the area by plane, taking it easy and trying to attract as little attention as possible. They dropped the pilot off where it was safe and then tried to marshal their determination.

Jensen was beating them. Henry Morgan was beating them. Hell, even the mercs were ahead. But those that came last often used the mistakes of those that led to pull themselves level, to force a lead, and then to win. More often than not it was a matter of staying power.

Crouch laid out the next map on the short grass of a tree-shrouded clearing. The plane was bobbing a few meters offshore and the woods were quiet and dense, decidedly tourist unfriendly. The team figured they could spend a little time here.

"Santa Catalina Island," the boss said, "was a small island rarely used along the Spanish Main. That said, Morgan recaptured it twice and killed quite a few enemies there. He could also use Santa Catalina as a layover point on the way to Panama. Now, there has to be a good reason for these particular islands, these particular maps, right?"

Caitlyn nodded. "Well yeah, since Morgan no doubt had a hundred secret places."

"And, so far, we've only discovered local keepsakes," Alicia said. "Maybe it's a long-gone sign that he felt remorse, and drew these maps to assuage his guilt. Return the locals' more sentimental riches and, if you're good enough, eventually find the hoard."

"Santa Catalina is a small place, uninhabited and, in those times, wasn't even connected to the mainland. There's now a one-hundred-meter footbridge connecting it to its big brother to the south, Providencia Island. Interestingly, we are now approaching the era of Morgan's life in which he started to lose England's support, eventually this would lead to him giving up the life of piracy—or privateering—returning to England, and later return as governor," Crouch shook his head. "Of Jamaica."

Alicia smiled without humor. "Three hundred and fifty years," she said. "And have we learned anything?"

"Best not to go there," Crouch said. "If I'm being truthful the history surrounding Morgan, or any pirate, and Santa Catalina is pretty thin, but it's safe to say he spent quite a bit of time there. And relatively alone."

The team studied the map a little more. Alicia took a few moments for herself, switching off and evaluating this new chapter in her life. The truth was, she was far from where she wanted to be. And for the first time in her life, far from where she felt belonged.

Never belonged anywhere before.

But comrades and friends needed her, whether most of them acknowledged it or not. Her new life with its new emotions and goals tugged furiously, but loyalty and honor had drawn her to Crouch and the others, and now it kept her there.

To the end. Bitter, or sweet.

"So where is it, this island?" she asked.

"In between Aruba and Jamaica." Crouch told her and held up a hand. "As the crow flies, that way."

"Not so long by plane," Healey said.

"Just try not to crash this time," Alicia said. "For a change."

"Hey, I don't fly that often."

"One out of one don't make me feel any better, kid."

"And stop calling me kid. Last time I checked, I was twenty five."

Alicia guffawed, unable to stop herself. The older members of their team turned knowing eyes upon the young soldier.

"I have to say," Alicia said as they packed up, stood up and walked toward their plane. "I'm not feeling the pull of the treasure on this one, boss. Not like the last two."

Crouch shrugged. "It's reality. This is how it is in the real world, I'm afraid. Following one rough clue to the next and hoping you don't reach that dead end. That point where all the clues and all the information runs out. We scramble around in the dark, Alicia, chasing old men's ancient ramblings, and occasionally get lucky."

"Wow, you shoulda gone into advertising with that outlook."

Crouch looked grimly to the skies. "Jensen has half a day head start. Let's move."

## CHAPTER EIGHTEEN

Another flight and another few hours behind them, and Alicia was starting to feel decidedly light-headed. Of course, the other option was riding the waves and that prospect excited her even less. Crouch plotted the course to Santa Catalina and called them all to the windows when the island drew close.

Alicia stared below once more, by now used to the sparkle shimmering off blue waves and expecting nothing less. The gentle roll of the seas lay unbroken below and she saw no sign of other vessels.

"The way Henry Morgan is portrayed," Caitlyn posited, "you would think he was king of the pirates."

Crouch glanced over. "It has been said before that there was once a great pirate council," he told them. "Though these days it's vehemently refuted. Probably rightly too. Pirates have been romanced in both their intellect and their dealings, but I daresay a few, like Morgan and Edward Teach and Calico Jack had the brains and the resources to put together a congress of sorts."

"Slightly different eras," Caitlyn said.

"Ach, only just." Crouch grinned. "Give a man a vision to hold on to."

"I guess he was a king of his time then," Caitlyn said. "I wonder what it was like growing up alongside his legend."

"Depends how true the stories are," Crouch said finally. "And we'll never know. We're close now, people."

Alicia put her face close to the window and ignored her light stomach. She quelled the need to return to everything that was new and held all new promise. She was loyal. She was a soldier and would fulfill her promise.

And, one day she would get Crouch properly alone.

Below, the steady glitter gave way to a large lump of gray hills and greenery, a couple of slices of beach to either side. They could quite clearly see the footbridge connecting Santa Catalina to its neighboring island. The misshapen mass looked deserted at this altitude, and Healey started to take the seaplane down.

"Wait," Crouch warned. "Take a tour first."

Healey corrected and sent the battered seaplane on a circuitous route around the island. Alicia saw his unspoken question and voiced it aloud.

"How do you make a slow-moving seaplane look unsuspicious, Michael?"

"Who knows? Act like sightseers."

"I guess we are, but what about the bullet holes?"

Crouch gave her a rare grin. "Flew over a military range?"

"They armed the seagulls," Caitlyn said.

"Caribbean hospitality," Russo finished.

Healey circled the island once and then again a few hundred feet lower. Features became more visible, the tops of jagged hills and the spread of the canopy; the hidden places a group might frequent; the density and danger of the rocks near the beach.

Small inlets scattered to the north and south.

A large seaplane off the coast.

"It has to be," Crouch said, squinting.

"We'll look bloody foolish if it's a local tour," Russo said.

"Healey, take her down around the side of that outcropping. We'll go over the top of the hill. Russo, don't forget this time we have the script."

"Ah, I'd forgotten that."

"To the leeward I resolve to stash that which sorely plagues. This time the rocks will tell their story and the rising tides a tale. But rarely when they're high, never again under sail. Never again. It is here, but fear you must. Peril awaits."

"It's the right side of the island," Crouch said.

"But there's no beach," Russo peered down as they passed over for the last time. "Just a dirty great chunk of cliff."

Alicia closed her eyes. "Ah, Russo, I guess it comes to us all."

"What?" A growl.

"Age and the loss of vision. You saw the dirty great chunk of cliff but not the sea cave at its base?"

"Sea cave? Shit."

Alicia tended to agree. "I don't mind a bit of swimming," she clarified. "But like I said, diving's for friggin' dolphins."

"That's why I figure we go over the top," Crouch said. "We might find another way in. Cave. Blowhole. Stream bed. Natural formation. It's a good bet, and we really need to come at Jensen in a way he least expects."

"He lost a lot of men in the last encounter," Caitlyn said.

"My guess—he has plenty left and they'll be even meaner."

Healey brought the seaplane down and taxied toward a break in the rock formations that led toward a sloping, mossy bank dotted with trees. Alicia clapped him on the back as the craft drifted to a stop.

"Progress."

"Nice pep talk. Thanks."

"Anytime, Zacko."

The team exited the seaplane, piled into a dinghy and made a slightly undignified but short run to shore. Alicia beached the boat and Russo tied it up. Ahead, trees provided cover and gloom-ridden shadows and a break from the heat. They pulled themselves up and then threaded a way between mossy trunks, unable to find any kind of path. The struggle was awkward for a while as the slope steepened. Alicia found herself hanging onto a tree and pulling Caitlyn up. After that the incline eased and they made better progress. The canopy of leaves above began to thin out, allowing specks and then larger spots of sunlight to dapple the trunks and branches.

Alicia made ready to replace her sunglasses as the tree line thinned ahead.

Crouch slowed and then knelt behind one of the bigger tree trunks. The vegetation ended rather abruptly about ten meters further on, giving way to smooth, hard gray rock. The rock was a plateau, stretching in all directions, a rolling plain of slippery, unbroken boulders. The formation ended in the distance in a pointed promontory. Alicia and Russo scanned the area. Alicia tapped Crouch on the shoulder.

"Let's go, boss."

The team eased their way out into the open. Alicia held her fully loaded handgun tightly. The rifle was out of bullets now but the handguns had plenty of reserve. No hidden figures became visible. Slowly, they picked their way across the rock, wary of the drop-offs to both sides. Alicia saw Crouch casting about, clearly hoping for a hole or passage into the rock below, but nothing presented itself.

Alicia began to grow a little despondent. This hunt was not as forthcoming as those that had gone before. It felt to her almost as if she needed to press the issue a little. Force it all out into the open. But then, that was her true nature.

Halfway to the far edge now and still they crept along, finding nothing. They kept low, conscious of the sea vistas opening up slowly to the east and west. As they crept nearer to the edge a low roar reached Alicia's ears, a roar that started to get louder and louder.

She stopped. Russo stared over at her, nonplussed. Crouch gave a little chuckle from behind.

"Get ready." It sounded like he was moving back.

"For wha—"Alicia started to say and then it happened.

The thunder increased in volume and the ground shook. Alicia swept the rocks with her vision, saw nothing. Then, directly ahead, a spout of water erupted skyward—a perfect jet of seawater. Like a fountain it shot high and then came back down, drenching everything around.

Which included Alicia and Russo.

Crouch laughed and so did Healey and Caitlyn, the young solider more so than the rest. Alicia turned to Crouch, her entire body dripping. "What the fuck? Why didn't you warn us?"

"No real reason. But I did think Healey might enjoy the spectacle."

Russo spread his hands.

Crouch shrugged. "Collateral damage?"

"Oh, there's gonna be." Alicia wiped the water from her eyes and shook herself, grateful now for the blazing sun. "Right after this mission's finished."

Crouch timed the fountain. It erupted again a few minutes later. After the second time he crawled forward with a flashlight and studied the shaft. Too narrow and dangerous to climb or jump into, he fell back to his haunches, disappointment written across his face.

"It's bloody useless."

Healey joined him. "We can hardly use the same way in they did."

"Of course, I realize that."

Caitlyn squatted at their side, face turned downward, balancing hard on the uneven surface so as not to get her blue jeans wet.

Alicia turned to Russo and mouthed: "Twenty seconds."

The big man grinned.

Crouch started to rise. Caitlyn took hold of his hand and pointed at an angle, right under the surface of the blowhole. "What's that?"

Crouch drew them all away as the blowhole exploded, sent Alicia a crafty look and then returned. "What did you see?"

"A natural tunnel running away from the blowhole," she said. "Doesn't seem terribly steep but it is narrow."

"And slippery," Healey added.

Crouch got down on his stomach to view it properly. "Guys," he said presently, happily. "I think we found our way in."

## CHAPTER NINETEEN

The passage was narrow at first. Alicia made her way down the blowhole, holding onto the sides to keep her balance and then angled her body into the offshoot of rock. She made her way down a few feet, careful of the water-drenched surfaces and then called the next person. This way, they could send in two people safely between each eruption of water and allow those two to get a firm hold to ward off the weak jet of water that fell into the new hole. The entrance was angled away from the blowhole spout, which was helpful, and warded off most of the powerful water. Alicia climbed steadily down, a foot at a time, grateful that the going was relatively easy. A rocky tunnel provided hundreds of hand and footholds. The way below was dark and unsure, though, and Alicia didn't want to use her flashlight.

No telling where the enemy were.

Surrounded by hard, dripping rock and the smell of seawater, they made their way downward in some kind of muted shadow realm. They could hear the lap of water from below, the rumble of thunder shooting up the other shaft. They could feel the wash of seawater passing them by. The minutes they spent in there felt like hours.

Near the bottom of the shaft everything opened out, the rock falling away. Alicia hung suspended for a moment before letting herself drop into two feet of standing water. Ahead lay an arrow-straight tunnel, whilst behind stood a mountain of rock.

There was enough room for everyone so she waited for the team to join her.

"Onward and steady," Crouch finally said.

Alicia led the way, stepping through the water and using one side of the tunnel for balance. It was a feat just walking in the dark; there was never a time when she knew the next step was safe.

"It's getting lighter up there," she said.

"Not sunlight though," Crouch whispered. "That's a flashlight."

Even more carefully they crept forward, approaching the artificial light and the end of this particular tunnel. Alicia hugged the left hand side of the passage as much as she could, approaching the last few feet of rock.

She stopped, checked the preparedness of the crew.

"We good?"

The nodding was perceptible, just. Alicia then bent low and put her head around the corner, letting her eyes adjust. The scene was a surprise, even worse than she'd been suspecting.

Jensen stood in shallow water at the center of a sea cave. The roof vaulted high above and the walls were lost behind wedges of jagged rock. Largely inhospitable then, it did have a wide rocky shelf to the far side upon which men, even now, were piling several packs of explosives.

Alicia swallowed drily. "Oh crap, that can't be good."

"What?" Crouch came up behind her. "What's going on?"

"It looks like they're getting ready to blow the far wall. And if I'm being honest it's not really a wall, just a pile of rocks."

"Fucking Neanderthals," Crouch growled. "There'll be nothing left."

Jensen watched impassively as half-a-dozen of his men scurried back and forth, laying small but full packs of dynamite, and unspooling wires. The men were rushing as if in answer to Jensen's urgency. The wall in question was over nine feet high and just as wide, a latticework of boulders fitted together like a bad jigsaw puzzle, held by time and weight and a build-up of growth.

"If you're gonna do something, make it quick," Caitlyn breathed.

"I don't think we have the time," Crouch said. "Jensen's already got his finger on the trigger."

The man clutched a black box in his fist. Alicia beckoned the rest of the team forward to look, since every single mercenary was involved with Jensen's new plan. She wondered why they had decided to blow this particular wall, though in truth it was the only one that appeared to be man-made.

"Is that his thinking?" Crouch wondered aloud and then softly intoned the script: "To the leeward I resolve to stash that which sorely plagues. This time the rocks will tell their story and the rising tides a tale. But rarely when they're high, never again under sail. Never again. It is here, but fear you must. Peril awaits."

"That which sorely plagues?" Alicia said. "Doesn't sound at all like treasure to me."

"As we said, maybe it's the locals' stash. He wants us to find that first."

"Well, he'd better hurry up appeasing himself," Caitlyn said. "Because this is the penultimate map. We're almost out of time, folks."

"Speaking of out of time . . ." Alicia watched as the mercs started scrambling away from the ledge, packs set in place. Jensen barely gave them enough time before shouting, "Fire in the hole!" and squeezing a button on the little black box.

An enormous explosion rocked the cave. Everything from huge chunks to small shards of boulder erupted from the wall. The shelf before it exploded too, spraying rock, and a curtain of water swelled around the cave. As the rock wall disintegrated, a huge wave of seawater poured in from the underwater sea cave next door. Alicia swore and moved backward in a hurry, tripping over Russo. The big man just wasn't fast enough, stumbling as the wall of water smashed into them. The team flailed and fought to hold on. Alicia went down to one knee, fingers grappling desperately to the rock wall. Caitlyn started to be swept away, but Healey snagged her, lost his grip and then they both skidded away amidst the swirling waters. In a few moments the great wave began to subside as it found the exits, and only ankle deep eddies were left churning around their legs. Alicia pushed Russo aside and struggled back down the passage.

Healey was leaning over Caitlyn, holding her up, the two cut and bruised but otherwise unharmed. Alicia hurried over to them.

"Ya picked a right time for a shag, guys."

Healey could barely speak, but handed Caitlyn over and collapsed onto his back. Crouch then waved down the passageway and made a hurry-up gesture.

Alicia hefted Caitlyn to her feet. "You okay? Talk to me."

"Yeah, yeah. Just give me a minute."

"Sorry, no can do. We gotta go."

Alicia helped Caitlyn back up the passage and Healey followed them to Crouch's side. What they saw ahead widened their eyes more than any underground explosion ever could.

A ragged hole now existed where the wall once had. Even as they watched, several more rocks gave in and fell from the top of the pile, shattering below. Mercenaries waited in a row as Jensen pushed past them, approaching the new cave. From her vantage point Alicia could see it was about the same size as their own, but quite dark, the only illumination leaching from their own. Jensen held out a hand.

"Torch."

To a man the mercs lit genuine, flickering torches; thick

shafts of wood wrapped in flammable bandages. Alicia shook her head. "Bloody fruitloops really do believe they're pirates."

"They're playing a part," Crouch said. "Wouldn't anyone that wants to get paid at the end of the week?"

"Depends on the part, boss. And the lead male."

"Yeah." Russo laughed. "If they're not called Chris, Johnny or Matt she's stone cold."

"Well, I might be able to handle a Rob if you fancy it."

"Woman, you ain't never handling me."

"We'll see." They watched the mercs in silence for a while as they followed their boss to the hole in the wall and tried to figure out a way to climb through. In the end Jensen threw a leg over the new gap and hauled himself over, unmindful of the risks. The flickering torches shed a smoky light and smelled of tar. The swathe of bright light admitted by the large entrance to the original sea cave dimmed and shimmered as it reached in vain for its new neighbor. Alicia breathed deep as she waited.

"Not liking this."

"Not much choice," Crouch said.

"Always a choice. We could take 'em all out right now."

"Not in cold blood, Alicia. We're the good guys, remember?"

Alicia said nothing, wondering how it was that an evident enemy always had to be given the benefit of the doubt. It seemed to her that they could end Jensen's threat right here and now, maybe even make the last map and treasure hunt less of a stressful proposition.

"Wait," Crouch said as the mercs made their way over the wall. "What the hell is that?"

Now Alicia saw it too, saw why Jensen risked his life, saw why the mercs all appeared so excited and up for it. In the second sea cave there lay a shipwreck, broken mast positioned at an odd angle, the curve of a timber hull just visible. Alicia saw the evidence and still barely believed her eyes.

"It's been there all this time?"

"Rotting through the centuries," Crouch said. "No telling what's left now. But if Morgan took the time to sink an entire ship in that cave you can rest assured it's an important find."

"So now can we kill Jensen?"

"Let's wait and let them do all the work."

"Ah." Alicia finally gave in. "Nice idea."

The last merc jumped beyond the wall, leaving the way clear for the Gold Team to follow. Ahead, the centuries-old pirate ship lay in wait, ready at last to give up its final secrets.

## CHAPTER TWENTY

A pirate galleon, of smaller size than the norm, lay on its side, broken and rotting and wallowing sadly in about three feet of water. The sea cave filled up several times a year but for now, during this season, the water sat stagnantly at its lowest level. The timbers were warped or shattered, sticking out like broken ribs. The masts drooped and what little tatters of sail were still affixed to the spars were barely recognizable. But the fact that Captain Morgan had actually left this ship here filled the mercenaries with excitement. Alicia watched them clambering excitedly and recklessly onto the ship, one at a time. Even from here she could hear the timbers groaning.

Crouch grated his teeth together. "Assholes. Don't they know the ship itself is a bloody treasure? One of Morgan's vessels, still here above water? Damn."

"How can you tell it's one of Morgan's vessels?" Russo squinted. "The colors? Size? Memory?"

"I guess we'll find out," Crouch answered without even a hint of sarcasm.

Jensen walked the planks carefully, waving his men back before they did any more damage. It took a while and a fair amount of careful prizing apart of already damaged timbers, but the mercs managed to board the vessel and search its innards. Several items were brought out and deposited on the rocks, but nothing of any major import.

Alicia and Crouch kept careful watch, hidden by the jutting array of rocks and brighter light behind them. In the end over a dozen mercs worked the ship and Jensen wandered from point to point, always questioning, always searching. In one hand he held a new torch, in the other a tankard full of neat rum. Swilling it down liberally, he soon grew more vociferous, though appeared none the worse for wear.

Time stretched and Alicia became conscious that afternoon at least must be here. They still had their packs, so took the time to drink and eat. Not once did any of the mercs approach the wall, but stayed focused on the new shipwreck and Jensen's orders.

Alicia beckoned Crouch aside. "Let Russo and Healey watch for a while."

"I really need to watch Jensen."

"They'll call us if anything happens. And, Michael, you really need to come with me."

She saw his eyes sharpen as he detected a note in her voice. Alicia led the way across the sea cave and toward the entrance. Careful at first, she found a rock to perch on where she could stare out the overhung entrance and across the startling blue seas.

"What is it?" Crouch asked quickly.

Alicia sighed softly. "I came here to help you, but that's not the only reason I came."

"I imagine it had to be a pretty compelling reason to leave Drake behind."

"Oh, it was. The trouble is—I believe I know you, Michael. You are one of only a handful of people on this planet that I fully trust. And I find it hard to . . . put something dark between us out there."

"Ah, well you've done it now. Might as well continue."

Alicia met the man's eyes and hers were bleak. "Beau said something before he died." Her mind's eye switched instantly back to that final struggle between them, when her old boyfriend had tried to kill the entire team. Crouch had initially recruited Beau for himself and helped ease his way into Alicia's primary team, but the Frenchman had always been a treble agent, working for a crazy enemy. In his last moments he had suggested that Crouch either knew, or forced it to happen that way.

Alicia said as much, watching the man she had always happily called boss.

"Is that what Beau said? I'm surprised."

"I mean, the man's clearly a liar, but . . ."

"He wanted out," Crouch said. "After he infiltrated the Pythian shadow organization and got close to the boss, then betrayed him, Beau wanted out. I forced him to stay with you guys, with team SPEAR, because I knew he would be useful."

Alicia weighed his words. "You *forced* him? How's that? Beau was nobody's doormat."

"Before he was an assassin, Beau was a mercenary. Before that a solider. Before that an interrogator. There are an awful lot of closets, entire dark rooms, in the head of a man who was once an interrogator. That job, that past, does not sit well." Crouch looked downcast, pained even. "I was privy to some of his secrets. And I knew some of the men, now powerful, that once sat in his chair."

Alicia blinked hard. "Jesus. You blackmailed him?"

"And eventually broke him," Crouch said. "It's my fault he turned back to the Pythian organization in the end and put you all at risk."

"At risk?" Alicia yelled. "That's some fucking understatement!"

Heads turned. Russo frowned over at her to stay quiet. Alicia gave him the finger.

Crouch nodded his head slowly. "We're all a consequence of our actions, I guess. I am sorry, Alicia, but not every choice we make is the best one."

She knew that, knew it better than most. What stung her was the new knowledge that Crouch had coerced Beau and he might have done the same thing to others. An unquestionable trust, when broken, was a fragile bond to mend, as delicate as a bird's wing. One thing was certain though, it would take time.

"Do you want to know more?" Crouch asked.

"No." Alicia turned away and drank in the uplifting sight of the shimmering waves. "You're best leaving it right where it is."

And then she caught sight of Healey waving them back.

Quickly she rose and, without a word or a glance in Crouch's direction, re-joined the team. At the new hole in the rock wall she peered carefully through and picked out Jensen.

"What's happening, boys?"

"Reality just broke this pirate party up big time. Jensen's now spitting bloody fire instead of rum. Come watch."

Alicia took it all in.

"He's a bastard! He's led us a merry dance! If he were alive right now I'd string him up myself!"

"They found nothing?" Alicia asked wonderingly.

"Another strongbox full of trinkets." Caitlyn smiled. "Morgan's 'that which sorely plagues' I believe."

"Local loot."

Jensen raved himself out and then drank more rum. His men stood around looking despondent, their torches still flickering but now drooping. Alicia shook her head at Caitlyn. "Why sink an entire bloody ship?"

"A symbolic gesture would be my guess. Learned pirate captains were full of them back in the day. Granted, most were bloody and violent, but perhaps this helped ease Morgan's guilt."

"A proper search of that ship under restricted conditions would have revealed the truth." Crouch came up at that point. "Something we'll never now get."

Jensen wavered, now ranting about the drawbacks and consequences of following the last of the maps to its final destination. The end of the search for Captain Morgan's treasure hoard. The strongbox he held in his hand went up in the air and was then dashed against the nearest array of rocks. It contents scattered everywhere as the sides burst.

Crouch almost cried out. The loss to history, the mindless ransacking, was an abomination to his lifelong way of thinking.

Alicia drew her gun. "We're gonna end this right now. Fuck letting 'em do all the work for us. Are you with me?"

Crouch was the first to follow. "All the way."

## CHAPTER TWENTY ONE

Alicia crept carefully through the gap, knowing the gung-ho offensive would really do them no good here. Without a sound she dropped into the new sea cave and waited for the rest of the team to join her. Only Caitlyn stayed on the other side, armed with a rifle and a laser sight. Healey eyed it dubiously but Crouch gave him a pat on the shoulder.

"Gotta let her get involved sometime."

Alicia watched Caitlyn move. There was a quiet confidence now in the girl that she liked, a growing ease of movement and competency that she recognized.

"Hey Healey," she whispered as they waited among rocks. "Maybe your training of Caitlyn is paying off after all."

Healey frowned, unused to compliments from the blond warrior. "Umm, thanks."

"And how's the other part of the *training* going?" Alicia wiggled her brows.

"Oh, piss off."

Crouch and Russo soon joined them and made ready. Alicia crept among the rocks until she could retain cover no more and then ran soundlessly toward her enemy. She counted twenty in number, plus Jensen, and then the first of them caught sight of her.

"Wha—" He raised a gun.

Alicia stopped him in his tracks, putting him down in a groaning heap. Others were turning, some reacting quicker than others. Alicia sprang among them, knowing it was of the highest importance to get close and stop them using their guns for fear of hitting a comrade. She chopped a pistol away, then sent the man into his neighbor, who slipped headlong on the slippery, rocky surface. She heard Russo fire twice and Crouch just once, dropping mercs. Healey grabbed a wrist a moment before its owner pulled a trigger, deflecting the bullet a few inches past his own skull. Alicia spun a man around and used another's bobbing ponytail to slam them together.

Dropping low, she cast around.

A boot slammed her side. She ignored the pain and caught its occupant behind the knees, pulling hard. The body came down beside her and she struck at the neck and groin and other vital areas. She wrenched a knife out of the man's belt before he could draw it, gave it back blade first and heard him grunt in agony.

On to the next. She saw Jensen still aboard the creaking shipwreck, now surrounded by three men. She remembered him mentioning three lieutenants—or rather *shipmates*—but couldn't remember their names. She saw another man spinning and then helped Healey prize one away from his neck. Russo fought hard to their right, bringing his size and strength to bear as he pushed and pulled and threw man enemy against enemy. Twice, the pop of a rifle rang out and unseen enemies fell. Caitlyn was watching their backs and picking off the worse threats.

But Jensen was no fool. Ex-SAS, he took time to evaluate the situation, the possible outcomes, and then his next move. Alicia, also ex-SAS, thought she knew how his mind would work. This location, Morgan's penultimate treasure site, again had yielded little of importance for the self-proclaimed pirate. With only one site remaining he would see only one real option.

The treasure *had* to be at the end of the trail, and Jensen could always hire more men.

The man was already moving his whip-thin, brawny frame in the direction of the underwater sea exit.

Alicia would try anything once, and often had. "You work for that guy? Look! He's already leaving you."

Several heads swiveled. Alicia already knew she'd never turn them to her side so she took advantage of the distraction and put them to sleep with measured blows. Russo helped and so did Healey, Crouch consistently moving to watch their backs. A couple of mercenaries took steps toward Jensen, their mouths moving.

Alicia chanced another look at the Englishman.

His lieutenants had already drawn guns.

"Shit!"

Shots rang out and men collapsed. Alicia dived for cover as Jensen's lieutenants took out those that openly questioned their boss. It was a criminal law, a mercenary law, an old pirate law. Men scattered and then regrouped. The fight fell into disarray.

Jensen's voice boomed over all.

"To the boats!" he cried.

## CHAPTER TWENTY TWO

Alicia sprang after the fleeing mercenaries, unwilling to allow them to leave.

One fell face-first in the shallows beyond the rocky ground. Another whirled to strike at her but she pushed him hard, sending him tumbling against the side of Morgan's old ship. Russo lifted another and introduced him more permanently to the rotting timbers, leaving him struggling above the water.

"New figurehead?" Alicia muttered.

"Well planted," Healey said.

Russo kept quiet, concentrating on the running mercs and, no doubt, trying to keep ultimate control of his rage.

Alicia pushed on. She jumped up onto the side of the ship and picked her way across the perished wood. A timber in front of her collapsed under a man's weight, trapping his ankle and making him fall. Alicia took that as a sign of righteousness and clubbed him into unconsciousness.

She looked up. A man approached.

"I'm Labadee," he said.

One of Jensen's lieutenant's, he came at her with a knife to slow her down. The first thrust was measured, designed to force a mistake. She didn't fall for it, but did have to stop her advance.

Labadee came again, a series of three quick slashes, and Alicia swerved around each of them, the last drawing a thin line of blood across the top of her right arm. The man's eyes shone with bloodlust. Alicia shook her arm, spattering him with red.

"That's all you're getting."

As he hesitated, looking like he might want to taste the droplets, Alicia waded in. A boot to the left knee, a punch to the ribs. Another strike of a leg and Labadee was twisting away, evading her blows but unable to bring the knife to bear. Alicia pressed it, but couldn't turn her back on Jensen and his other men. Labadee pulled away.

Then Russo landed beside her, boots splintering timbers. A merc leapt at the big man, tripped over a jutting spar and went sprawling. Alicia wrestled a log free and hurled it at Labadee. The man didn't move, allowing it to strike his face and then licking his lips with a grin.

Alicia wasn't impressed. "Stay right there. I can probably fit the next one in yer gob."

Labadee opened his mouth.

Alicia ripped a chunk of timber free and sprang at the man. He was ready, striking out with the flat of the blade and then the tip. Alicia caught it deftly with the wood and then twisted, tearing it right out of his hands and trying to break his wrist in the process. Labadee let go quickly, backing up. Alicia sidestepped, but then Russo lunged too and splintered a little more of the ship. A man fell through a gap ahead, crying out with shock as he vanished into the bowels. Another man stepped onto a rotten spar and saw the bottom half of his body plummet until he wedged against his belt, left dangling and unable to wrench himself free. Jensen headed for the stern of the ship.

Alicia trod more carefully. The entire ship was groaning now, and she sensed it beginning to shift. Crouch was trying to skirt the vessel by using the rocks along the side, but the process was dangerous and slow. Healey looked like he didn't know where to put his feet. A merc turned to take a potshot at the lad, but Caitlyn took him out.

"Keep moving!" Alicia shouted.

The ship's prow buckled and fell with a deep grinding sound and a great splash of water. Timbers collapsed upon each other and several planks heaved themselves upward like spears. Alicia saw the crack tearing its way down the length of the galleon.

"Oh fu—"

She sidestepped, leapt away from the tear. Several mercs saw it coming and, to their credit, only one stayed there staring in confusion. He didn't hang around for long, plummeting the moment the running crack passed him by. The ship split apart, spars grating and groaning in resistance and in protest. Alicia felt herself overbalancing, but managed to compensate. Russo was not so nimble, nor so lucky. As the lower portion rolled so did the big solider, slipping, scraping and splashing into the deeper water.

Alicia made sure he was okay before letting a riposte come to mind, but by then Labadee was back in her face, and he'd brought a friend.

"Forrester," the man said. The second of Jensen's lieutenants.

"I don't give a shit," she said. "You assholes come any closer, you'll find out what it's like to get keelhauled."

They hesitated. Alicia caught a glimpse of Jensen leaping into the water and swimming hard for the small cave exit. Several mercs were at his side. The rest were pretty thinned out. Crouch struggled with a man close to the water's edge and Russo was busy swimming for a rocky shore. Healey waited at Alicia's side.

Labadee then saw the red dot hovering around his chest.

Most men's reaction would be to turn and dive, but the Jamaican only stopped and searched out the source of the dot. He found Caitlyn hidden among the rocks and gave a crooked grin.

"You people, you're cleverer than you look."

Alicia coughed. "And you're not only stupider, but uglier too."

Labadee frowned a little at that before holding out both palms and backing up. Forrester went with him, the man's blond curls tightly wrapped to his bronzed skull.

They jumped into the water just as Russo climbed out. Alicia gave the surprised soldier a shake of the head.

"I've seen faster seahorses, Rob. Really I have."

"I don't know if that's good or bad."

Healey helped him out. "Alicia said it."

"Ah, then fuck you too, bitch."

Crouch was waving wildly at them. "What are you all waiting for? We have them on the run! Let's bloody well end this."

## CHAPTER TWENTY THREE

Beneath the calm waves there lay a quiet, confused world of drifting bodies, shattered timbers and more than one glinting bauble. Visibility was average though and allowed Alicia to pinpoint the exit as she swam closer. There was the brief kicking of heels ahead, underwater splashes, and then the last of the escaping mercs was gone. She struck out faster, hating the below-sea-level environment, but more concerned about her safety than her wishes at that point. The rest of the team were close by, bruised but still ready to fight.

The exit was little more than a narrow cave entrance, barely wide enough to accommodate the small galleon that Alicia assumed must have been sailed in during one of the few times a year it was accessible. Moss hung across the entrance and slithered across her skin as she swam by. Her lungs burned steadily, needing to breathe. Once through she arrowed up toward the surface, embracing the light that brightened with every kick of her legs. Crouch got there first and then Healey, but finally Alicia breached the surface.

Letting the water drip from her face, clearing her eyes, she quickly evaluated the ever-shifting horizon. Jensen's white seaplane was anchored offshore, just as they'd spotted it from the air. Many pairs or arms swam toward it now, cutting hard through the clear, blue waters. The sun beat down relentlessly, already starting to dry the droplets on her skin. Alicia took a deep, sweet breath.

Russo started a strong crawl in pursuit of the men. By chance the plane lay close to a rock promontory and it appeared most of the mercs were making for dry land first rather than the plane. Maybe they had stashed gear there, or had taken boats from the main island since there were surely too many bodies for the plane alone.

That said, it wouldn't surprise Alicia if Jensen hadn't strapped a few to pontoons, wing struts and any other surface he could think of.

The Gold crew struck out for the rocks, staying low but keeping their weapons as much out of the water as possible. Sometimes they had to be submerged and should still work fine, but there was no reason to tempt fate. Russo aimed for a point behind the mercs as they scrambled out of the water, finding it hard to gain purchase on the saturated rocks, some falling back and others cracking their heads and bruising bones.

Alicia gathered her breath. "Steady on, Robster. Looking at those guys, you're about to experience a calamity."

"Once." Russo shook his head. "I misjudged once."

"And you'll pay for it forever," Healey said.

"One more comment and I'll have your ass, Myles."

"Ooh, promises, promises. Just name the place and position."

Russo choked on seawater, head momentarily going under. Crouch hit the rocks first, found purchase, and pulled himself up. Healey helped Caitlyn and then Russo approached the jagged pile.

Alicia swam at his back, waiting.

"Wanna hand? A well-placed finger will have you squealing to the top of that pile in half a second."

"Just stay away."

The soldier heaved himself out and then Jensen's men spotted them. Guns were drawn and shots fired. Crouch and the others took cover behind the rocks and started to creep forward. Alicia trod water for a while, watching the scene with frustration.

Why the hell didn't I just jump out? Now I'm stuck her whilst the guys face a firefight. You're such an idiot, Myles.

It all reminded her that she was in the crux of a big change, but some things were destined to remain exactly the same.

As if she'd ever stop taking the piss!

The rock cover was good, and the ways between them slippery but safe. The mercenaries were more concentrated on escape than confrontation, and soon began diverting their attentions to the plane and inflatables that lay tethered to the rocks. Alicia used the distractions to climb quickly out and shrug off a waterfall.

"Bloody Alsatian in more ways than one," Russo muttered.

Alicia eyeballed the man. "You'll pay hard for that."

"Already am, Myles. Already am."

The staggered, haphazard firefight continued steadily, the Gold Team creeping ever nearer. The mercs began to thin out and Alicia saw Jensen and his nearest cronies board the seaplane. She saw he had a further half dozen mercs with him who started to tether themselves to the plane. She lined up a shot, but at this distance with a handgun it was a useless effort. Better to keep the bullets.

The seaplane started up at the same time as several of the outboard motors belonging to the inflatables. Alicia took out another merc but the rest were already aboard and waiting for the escape.

She saw it all coming down to the last map.

Jensen took off and veered around in the air, coming above them and holding both hands out of the window. The rest of the doors stayed shut and then Jensen's face popped out into the open.

Alicia had him dead to rights, but knew she couldn't fire. Only criminals did that. The good guys had to wait to be fired upon first.

"You murdered more than half my crew! For no reason! You won't leave me be! I'll come for you all, believe me. After Morgan's treasure I'll be concentrating all my efforts on you and yours! I'll wipe all of you out!"

The face pulled back and the plane went on its way. Some of what Jensen said was torn away by the winds but Alicia got the general gist.

"What a knob."

Russo took a rock pew, wiping his face. "So what next, guys?"

"Panama City." Crouch grimaced. "It was the last place Morgan sacked before returning to England where he thought he'd die. It's the last map."

## CHAPTER TWENTY FOUR

Panama City—arguably one of the most important cities throughout history. It was from here that the Spanish launched their expeditions to conquer the Inca empires of Peru. A transit point for untold wealth headed back to Spain. Beyond that, the canal, and the time that Captain Henry Morgan put fire to and destroyed the entire city. Alicia knew a little of the histories, the embellished ones and the much starker realities. What concerned her was the absolute size of the place, and the fact that Morgan practically razed it to the ground.

Their chartered jet bore them steadily through the clear skies.

"Now Michael," she said. "Without meaning to be a bitch I do have to point out the vagueness and shoddy skills inherent in your mapmaking. They're shit, and Panama City's a pretty big place."

Russo stared at her. "That's *not* being bitchy?"

"Not even a little bit."

Alicia watched Crouch's face. The cave battle had interrupted their eye-opening conversation about Beau, and she was still processing the details. But she hadn't liked what she heard. It showed a different side to Crouch—and the possibility that she'd read yet one more person incorrectly.

"Mapmaking skills aside," Crouch said. "There is also the script, little though I remember of the final map, and the fact most of the city is comparatively new."

"Morgan destroyed it," Alicia said bluntly.

"Panama is where it all finally went wrong for Morgan,"

Caitlyn spoke up. "He ended up having to divide his forces and march through forest and village to attack the fort, arriving starving and hounded by the Spanish. Forewarned, almost all of the potential treasure hoard had been loaded onto a galleon prior to his arrival and sailed out to sea. The pirates then decided to drink and carouse in Panama rather than use their superior nautical skill to chase down the ship. The city was put to flame." Caitlyn shook her head sadly.

"A bad night for the pirates," Russo said unnecessarily.

"It got worse," Caitlyn said. "The sack of Panama broke the peace treaty between England and Spain, although it could be argued Morgan had no knowledge of the treaty at the time. In any case, his arrest was called for and Morgan had to return to his home and then the capital city to answer for his crimes."

"He survived though as I remember?" Alicia frowned.

Caitlyn shrugged. "Oh yeah, the English knighted him."

"All that aside," Crouch spoke up as the others considered Caitlyn's statement. "The new Panama City was built five miles west of the original city. Today the old town is called Panama La Vieja, essentially Old Panama."

"How much of the place still stands?" Alicia asked dubiously.

"Not much," Crouch admitted. "So let's hope it's enough."

Alicia made her face a little glum. "And a fine bloody treasure hunt this is. No gold, no prospects and very little enthusiasm. The only thing we have gained is a lot of bruises."

Russo shifted in his seat. "Sounds like you're getting old, Myles."

Alicia considered his words. "Until a certain age you don't care about age. But there comes a point when you decide that you *want* to get old. Understand?"

"No more carefree, live or die, death-defying assaults? You talk like someone that has kids." Russo turned to her with wide eyes. "You're not bloody pregnant are you?"

Alicia choked and coughed so hard it hurt her lungs. She couldn't speak for a minute and then looked up to see four wry grins.

"Oh, bloody funny. Pick on poor Alicia why don't you."

Russo made a finger sign in the air as if to say 'one point'.

Alicia nodded. "That's two I owe you, Rob."

The jet banked and started to descend. Within a half hour they had bumped down the runway, tasted the hot air of Panama, and were waiting at customs. The team had brought only their civilian packs for ease and speed of movement, but Crouch knew someone in the city that could help them obtain weaponry. Once clear of the airport the team rented an SUV to take them into the heart of Panama City, threading through the high rises and along the flat, wide roads, taking a route that enabled them to identify any tail. The going was good and Crouch soon told Healey to stop the car whilst he made contact with his local acquaintance. Alicia watched the boss through the recently cleaned windows as he chatted and laughed in the shadows of a warehouse doorway. In essence nothing had changed, but somewhere deep inside a seed of suspicion had been planted. She still had no doubt that Crouch was essentially a good man, but not quite the role model she had imagined.

After a few moments he beckoned toward Healey, and the young solider backed the SUV up to a discreet doorway. Russo climbed out and helped Crouch load a couple of holdalls into the back. Alicia watched the street, the rooftops, all bleached by the sun, the windows that faced their way and the street corners. The area was quiet, which was of course why the dealer had picked it.

They continued without incident, now threading their way through the city and toward the old quarter, now called Casca Viejo. The original city was built on a peninsula, surrounded by the sea and an easily defended wall system.

Alicia settled back until Crouch stopped the car and spoke up. "We should get out here and walk. Play tourist. There are a few ruins back there—" he pointed "—most importantly a sixteenth-century cathedral."

"And why so important?" Alicia asked.

"Because the pirates spent time there and it was mentioned as a landmark on the map."

The team exited the car and stepped out into the blazing sunshine. "The Welsh pirate, Henry Morgan," Crouch said, looking around and sniffing the air as if he might be able to conjure the scent of smoke and gunpowder, "found an end to his pirating days here. I wonder if the English hadn't recalled him would he have quit anyway?"

"Hard in those days to be a captain and a quitter," Russo pointed out. "The crew would have lynched him."

"Good point," Crouch said. "And what to do with all that treasure?" He stopped in the middle of the sidewalk and looked around. "What indeed?"

Alicia took in their surroundings. Casca Viejo seemed to be a small town with a neatly laid-out collection of buildings, several narrow through roads and sea views to most sides. Crouch input the coordinates to the cathedral on his Android phone and started to follow the resulting blue line and soft-spoken directions. The town appeared quiet, but several people wandered the streets or drove their cars along the roads. Another sleepy place then, just like most they had visited in the last few days.

"All right, I admit," Alicia said as they walked. "I couldn't handle all this chilled-out stuff. I'd go nuts."

Russo joined her at the back of the team. "In some ways it would . . ." He struggled to speak the word, even a simple one. "Help."

Alicia sensed the big soldier might finally have something to say. "Is the rage so bad?"

"Imagine a matchstick sparking to life. Imagine a pile of tinder set aflame. Then see it spread into a forest fire that engulfs a state. That's the rage. And you feel it every day."

"No diminishing?"

"Sometimes." Russo shrugged slightly. "Depends on the day."

"When did you first feel it?" She knew it was an important question and one Russo might not want to answer.

"I can't remember when it wasn't there."

Alicia was surprised. "Really? Earliest memory? School?"

"Yeah. A bigger boy decided to bully me. They had to pick his arms and legs up off the floor." Russo frowned. "Figuratively."

"And the source?"

Russo was silent for a time. "Ah, I'm not ready for that yet."

Alicia nodded. "So why now? Why tell me now, I mean?"

"I sense the change in you. Out of all the people I know, you'll handle the truth best."

Alicia nodded toward Crouch. "Better than the boss?"

"He wouldn't understand. You will. And we have the battle trust now."

Soldiers that faced death together bonded fast. Alicia already felt she could ask Russo anything. The answer, however, might come pricklier than a briar patch but as Russo said—she could handle anything.

"I'll be ready. But look—is it better to hold it all in, or to just let it go?"

"I understand why you ask that. You'd think venting the rage would make it all easier. But in fact it's the opposite. Opening the cage only makes it want more."

"And talking about it?"

"I guess we'll see."

Russo moved off, walking up front and saying no more. Alicia took a few moments to study the Gold crew, thinking about how they came together and how well they worked as a team. This quest, with all its disappointments and dead-ends and nasty pieces of work pitted against them was more than testing, more than mystifying, it was a way of building up the team.

Healey strode along beside Caitlyn, the two not touching but clearly wanting to, happy together and less vigilant because of it.

But Alicia watched out for both of them. She studied Crouch too, and wondered if there were more secrets to come. *Could there be worse?*

It didn't matter. Because they were a team. When it came down to it, Alicia would risk everything for every one of them. Crouch then stopped up ahead, staring at a row of trees.

Time to go to work.

## CHAPTER TWENTY FIVE

Alicia found herself entering a pleasant, peaceful area bordered by trees. Well-tended lawns were broken only by a few narrow gravel paths. Low, ruined walls ran everywhere and could have been the remnants of almost anything, but one tall brick tower still stood at the far end of the site.

Alicia stopped. "That's a cathedral?"

Crouch nodded. "Apparently. Destroyed by an earthquake in 1644. Rebuilt only to be set upon by Morgan—and others—since. Maybe they knew it wasn't destined for a happy life."

Alicia studied the single tower with its empty windows and crumbling frames. The top tier was blackened, as if still bearing the stains of the seventeenth-century ravishing, but Alicia knew it couldn't be so.

Could it?

"Is this site still in use?"

"Only for tourists. I did think there would be more of them around right now, considering the time."

Alicia guessed mid-afternoon was a good visiting time, but the area was empty. Tranquil, but eerily so as if a four-hundred-year-old ghost had chased everyone away. Crouch stared hard at the cathedral itself.

"I guess we should start there."

Russo fell in line. "Is this a good time to ask what the script actually said?"

Crouch fished out the map. "Well, as we know this was a bad venture for Morgan and his band of pirates. Missed out on the gold. Arrived starved and desperate after days of being ambushed through the woods. Allegations of torture and still no gold. Then the great fire, which some say was set by Morgan and others that the town's captain general ordered the gunpowder magazines exploded. Either way, thousands died. And so we come to the ruins of *Nuestra Senora de la Asuncion*. And so to Morgan: 'Our woes and our fate and our comeuppance came all at once in the City. Our reward gone, our hearts and heads all ablaze with rage, we blamed the town. And its people. Shame on us. And what recompense we could make, we made at Nuestra.'"

"Ahh," Healey said. "Now it makes sense. I couldn't understand the connection between the cutthroat Morgan and a house of God." He paused. "Except maybe the charring."

Alicia kept her eyes on their perimeter. "Let's hope there's an X this time. Burned into the ground."

"Amazing it's stood so long," Caitlyn said. "And became part of a World Heritage Site."

Alicia saw a shape flit between the trees. Not the slow meanderings of a tourist, but the quick gait of a man coming closer. The sighting was too quick to make out if he carried a gun, but she reached down for hers.

"Nine o'clock," she said. "Potential enemy."

Russo nodded. "And at eight. We're being watched."

Crouch folded the map. "We're twenty feet from the cathedral. Can we make it?"

"If that's around eight meters," Healey again showed his youth, this time on purpose, "then I think we can."

Alicia dropped to one knee and drew her weapon. "Then go," she muttered. And then, loudly, she called, "Show yourselves, boys. Best to stay on my good side."

As the team headed rapidly for the dark, open doorway, Alicia saw three men leap out into the open. Instantly, she registered they carried weapons, and opened fire. Distance affected her aim and the bullets shot wide, but still caused enough consternation to give her a little more time.

She backed up, following her team.

Russo spun at the cathedral entrance and squeezed off a few more shots. More men appeared among the trees. Alicia quickly counted five before joining Russo.

"Why an ambush?"

The big soldier shrugged. "Maybe they were waiting for us to find something. Maybe we saw 'em sooner than we should. We need to—"

Crouch's yell of warning cut him off. "More here!"

"Crap." Alicia bypassed Russo, leaving him on guard at the door, and headed inside. The cathedral smelled of age and mold, heat and dark places. The alcoves were covered in cobwebs. Steady rays of sunlight beamed through the open windows above, a golden latticework, shot through with dust motes. She could already see the building's far exit and Crouch leaning against an ancient wall as three men picked themselves up from the floor ahead. They carried shovels and backpacks, flashlights and pistols.

Alicia lined them up. "Hold up. Don't move."

Hard faces stared back at her, but nobody moved. The men stood holding their various implements.

Crouch waved his gun at them. "Drop 'em."

"C'mon, man," an American voice drawled. "She told us to stay put. Who's in charge around here? The skirt or the dude?"

Alicia fired a bullet through the gap in between his legs. "Call me a skirt again and the wedding veg come off."

The grim exterior suddenly became a pale wreck. "Um, yeah, no worries..."

Crouch emerged as the men clearly recalculated. It was unlucky then that, from another alcove, a gun appeared.

Alicia shouted. Healey, behind her, fired. The distraction gave the three diggers chance to make their moves. Healey's bullet glanced off the brick wall, sending sharp shards into the owner of the gun and forcing him to drop it. Alicia shot into the body mass of the first digger as he drew a weapon and the other two leapt away, dragging their packs after them.

Russo shouted down the short passageway. "We may have a problem here."

Alicia grunted. "We ain't exactly chatting over tea and biscuits, Rob."

"Yeah? Do they have anti-tank missiles?"

She stayed calm. "Oh, I don't know, let me ask one of them."

Her bullet missed by millimeters.

Crouch was staring at her, clearly concerned and shocked. "Looks like Jensen's following up on what he said. He now wants us as badly as he wants the treasure."

"Shit."

Alicia waved Healey and Caitlyn past and into cover and then paced back down toward Russo and the cathedral entrance. Staying flat against the wall, she peered out. She counted eight now, two of whom carried rocket launchers. The rest looked to be toting the usual collection of AKs and H&Ks but she thought she spied several hand grenades too.

"Looks like Jensen has access to the proper hardware after all."

"So now you believe me?"

"Oh stop panicking. It's only a fucking rocket launcher. We've faced far worse."

"Only . . ." Russo shook his head. "Shit, Myles, what the hell is it like to be inside your head?"

"Not as much fun as being inside my pants. But hey, we'll save that for later." Alicia considered trying to pick off the RPG-carrying men, but couldn't be certain what their orders might be. Fire if fired upon? And there were other men who might pick the weapons up. She held off, watching their progress.

"You think they set this up as an ambush?"

Russo grunted. "Had to be. Jensen knew we'd come and they're prepared. I just wonder what his overall aim is. Aren't we at the final clue?"

"Looks like he's given up on Morgan's booty. And now he's after ours."

Alicia watched the approaching men and read their patterns. Soon they would come within an acceptable range. Behind, shots rang out and Crouch yelled for the enemy to stand down. Only a volley of gunfire greeted his call.

"See you on the other side, Robster."

Surprisingly, she ran out into the open, gun up, but she knew what she was doing. One of the low, ruined walls afforded good cover and it gave her and Russo a much better line of sight. She skidded in, dropping low and kept her head down as a salvo of bullets smashed into the old bricks. The grass was bone dry and emanated an earthy smell this close to her nose. With an eye on Russo she waited for his nod, then inched her head up and carefully squeezed off three rounds. One man fell dead. Another twisted, wounded in the shoulder. She ducked as men returned fire, but then Russo opened up and felled another.

Already they were down to five and one wounded.

Alicia rolled further down the length of the wall. Russo signaled that a man was running at her but then had to duck inside as men turned weapons upon him. She slithered a bit further and then rose, gun aimed steady.

She experienced a shock. The man coming for her at full pelt held one of the grenade launchers and it was loaded. Before Alicia could do anything, he loosed the missile at the place she had originally been. Alicia had seconds to roll even further, then tucked her body into the fetal position, hugging the wall as closely as possible. An explosion rocked the entire site. A plume of black earth and shattered brick blasted past the side of the cathedral.

Alicia still gripped her gun, and felt the blast wave pass by. The direction of the explosion was at a right-angle to her, so none of the deadly debris came close. But earth, grass and fragments of brick soon began to rain down.

In the midst of it, Alicia rose and fired hard into the mass of her attacker. The rocket launcher flew high and he flew straight back, blood erupting from his chest. Behind him came another man, this one toting a rifle, and Alicia took him down with a single headshot.

Three remaining, one wounded.

Alicia ducked once more, head pounding and ears ringing from the explosion. The shattered earth lay to her right, a black swathe of destruction delved from the cathedral's hallowed grounds. She wondered briefly if Jensen was there and where he might be hiding.

A thought occurred.

Then, Crouch and the others came sprinting out of the cathedral. Alicia hesitated, caught between necessities, but her team came first. Crouch was already seeking her out.

"Lots more of them round back," he shouted, face scared. "Too many."

Healey followed, pushing Caitlyn hard. Bullets fizzed past them, striking brick and stone, and blasting through empty air. So many impact dust plumes sprang up that a gray cloud swirled through the air. Russo, forced out of cover, joined the wild sprint, now all out of options.

Alicia felt a blast of desperation. No way could they all sprint like that together and not take a bullet. It was a matter of seconds, a wild card race. She could only guess at how many mercs gave chase, but she knew it was a damn sight *too* many.

Without a moment's hesitation, without any doubt, she put

the team first. Lunging over the wall, she kicked the dead merc aside and hauled up his missile launcher. A man fired at her and she returned the bullet with her left hand, hefting the metal tube with her right.

Then she dropped her own gun, wrenched a grenade out of the merc's backpack and loaded the launcher.

She sighted on the ancient cathedral.

And pulled the trigger.

## CHAPTER TWENTY SIX

Crouch, Healey, Caitlyn and Russo ran headlong and desperately away from Panama Viejo's centuries-old cathedral, moving so fast they were practically tripping themselves and finding it hard to balance. Bullets created a tracery among them. Lady Luck shone her bright light. But even that would not have been enough if Alicia hadn't acted within seconds. Healey felt fire along his leg, saw Crouch stumble as a lead missile cut through the strap of his pack. It was that close.

Then, to his left, Healey saw Alicia's intention.

*Fuuuuuu...* ran through his head even as he ran for his life.

With Caitlyn directly before him and flat even ground, he turned his head to watch as Alicia depressed the rocket launcher's trigger and let loose the grenade. A streak of white smoke denoted the bomb's trail and then it struck the side of the cathedral with stunning force. The entire wall buckled. A hole blasted through the side. An explosion rocked the dying day. Healey leaped as the entire structure wobbled.

He heard Alicia's groan: "Ah, shit."

The lower part of the tower came down in a cascading, fragmented shale whilst the top half collapsed to the right, groaning as it leaned and then fell, its last moments becoming a roar and then a blast like a detonation. Smoke and dust marked its final resting place and the graves of the mercs that had been chasing Healey. The entire team slowed as they were then faced with three gun-toting mercs.

Alicia was already sprinting their way.

Healey pulled Caitlyn to the side as he lifted his gun and fired in one swift movement, leaping left. The action sent the mercs scrambling and Caitlyn flying, but it helped gain them precious extra moments. Healey had been a badly bullied younger brother until he joined the Army at the age of eighteen. Now, he reveled in the new experience and the incredible responsibility. He hit the grass and rolled, rose fast, took a punch to the jaw because he hadn't reckoned on the proximity of his opponent. Rookie mistake. He survived it, though, stumbling on purpose, creating space and shooting the man. Alicia was then at his heels.

"C'mon, Zacky, stop praying. The bloody cathedral's gone."

*Funny.* He stood up and immediately looked for Caitlyn. She was struggling on her haunches as a merc strode toward her, pointing his gun. Caitlyn couldn't raise hers and Healey set off on an impossible sprint, screaming, "No!" as he went.

The merc grinned.

Caitlyn turned her eyes to Healey.

No.

Russo came out of nowhere, hitting the merc with a rugby tackle that almost broke him apart at the waist. The gun went flying, the man's headset too as he all but folded in half. Russo pounded down as he landed, the arms descending like a full-size gorilla's upon a small animal, breaking bone and shattering teeth with every strike. He would not stop. He could not stop. The rage was a living thing that encompassed all and sent the world away for a time. Healey helped Caitlyn up and then raced over to Russo.

"Rob, stop! You're killing him." He tried because he knew Russo would regret it later, only for his teammate. He got in close and risked a battering.

"It's not worth all the self-loathing, mate," he said quietly. "Not this brain-dead animal."

Russo flung arms down twice more. The merc's face was bloody, misshapen. Alicia arrived at that moment. Russo hesitated with his fists in mid-air, blood dripping down, and drew in a deep, wracking breath.

"Oh, hell. Oh, bloody hell."

He collapsed face first beside the unconscious figure, rasping for air and coughing at the same time. Healey moved in but Alicia held up a hand.

"Let me."

He delayed, allowing Caitlyn to draw him away. It was easy to forget that Alicia, having overcome some major crisis of her own recently, was fast becoming a deeper, more caring person and trying to help in every way she could. The more she succeeded the more she would try.

Healey draped an arm around Caitlyn's shoulders. "I was worried there."

"You didn't see Russo. That merc never stood a chance."

"Still . . . it was too close."

"Aw, still looking out for me?"

"Always."

She hugged him briefly. Healey allowed her that few moments even as he cast around for what they should do next. Caitlyn would need the close companionship even if they weren't together. Her recent move to the Gold Team had been due to an early-twenties burnout. Devastating, and all down to the revelations surrounding the fact that her father beat and killed her mother. A lifetime of love could never put that knowledge to the side, but Healey would be happy to try.

Crouch had now finished off the last merc. He glanced over to their little party. "Is Russo aware?"

Healey knew he was questioning how deep the rage-state had affected the soldier. Healey caught Alicia's eye.

"All good?"

Alicia blinked. "Give me a few."

Healey held up three fingers. Crouch nodded and then started to survey the area.

"We have to find Jensen," he called over. "Did they find anything? And this will never be over until he's out of the picture. Not for us."

"Sorry?" a British accent called out. "Did someone mention my name?"

## CHAPTER TWENTY SEVEN

Alicia didn't move a muscle, but studied the scene from beneath hooded eyes. Jensen had finally emerged from around the side of the devastated cathedral, four men flanking him. All had machine pistols trained on the Gold Team. Jensen staggered a little, still clutching what looked like a bottle of rum in one hand and a Glock in the other. The gun faced the floor whilst the bottle's rim approached his lips.

"Well, here I am." He swallowed deeply and wiped his chin. "Come get me."

Russo stopped breathing, constantly trying to get a grip on his anger. Alicia reviewed the options. It was a short list. They still had their weapons, but without a distraction some of them were going to die.

Crouch walked steadily toward Jensen. "What did you find?"

The Englishman took a moment to turn an ironic eye upon the fallen, still smoking building. "Would you believe—nothing at all?"

"I'd say you were full of shit."

A shrug. "No matter. We found the usual—a strongbox full of trinkets that are worth nothing at all."

Crouch sighed. "But of course they're worth something to someone, that's the whole point of what Morgan has been doing here."

"Eh?" Jensen raised the plastic bottle and drank some more.

"Don't you see? This is his atonement. Only a pirate could express his regret this way and only Morgan did it. These treasures, returned to their rightful owners—are a four-hundred-year-old act of contrition."

"You're saying Morgan became a pussy?"

Crouch continued to engage Jensen as his team moved inch by inch to attain better positions. An elbow moved here, a knee there, a better grip on the pistol. A clear way in which to roll. A better line of sight. The minutes passed and the odds lessened.

"You never committed an act you regret?"

Jensen shrugged. "Plenty."

"And you never tried to atone." Crouch was now between his team and two of the shooters. Alicia silently berated him for such idiocy.

"You can't take it back," Jensen spat. "And they never, ever believe you. You take what you can in this life, Crouch, and you *never* give back."

"Spoken like a criminal."

"Maybe. But this criminal outsmarted you and is about to kick your damn ass."

"Maybe . . ." Crouch let it hang.

Tension fell over the cathedral grounds like a thick blanket, cancelling out any other noise. The thin air itself seemed to curdle with a jittery energy. Nobody wanted to die that day, but nobody wanted to back down either.

Alicia moved first, decision made minutes ago and as good as she was going to get. She fell flat alongside Russo, sheltered somewhat by the dead mercenary's body and pulled her trigger. At the same time two of the four mercs shot at them, bullets slamming hard into the dead flesh, shooting up two separate red mists. Alicia didn't flinch, but kept firing. Her second bullet found her target's chest, her third his heart and he was falling away.

Alicia ducked as a line of ammo stitched across their shield. She dug in closer, head below his body and pushed against the grass. Russo returned fire but the rage had left pockets of fiery adrenalin within him that appeared to be affecting his aim.

Healey had body-slammed Caitlyn out of the way; she landed among the fallen cathedral's stones and struck her head, but the swift movement saw bullets pass them by. The only person that didn't move at all was Michael Crouch.

Nobody fired on the boss. Alicia never knew for what reason; she assumed because he was the object of conversation for Jensen, but his position between two shooters and Healey and Caitlyn helped save their lives.

Jensen raised the Glock.

Crouch bounded, still fleet of foot despite his age, and caught Jensen's gun hand. The two came together struggling hard. Ex-SAS training brought to bear on both sides, and neither was better. Both men fell to their knees.

Alicia wrenched her eyes away from the individual battles and focused on her own. Russo had finally started to focus, and wounded their opponent. Alicia jumped upright and emptied her magazine into the man before he could react further. Russo followed her. Over to the right, Healey and Caitlyn slipped among the rubble, falling hard as more shots rang out. The shots arrived a moment later than both Alicia's and Russo's however, so ended up being aimed at the clouds as the shooters fell over backwards, already dead.

Alicia put two slugs into the dirt beside Jensen's left knee.

"Game's up, fool."

She didn't add but thought: *At last.*

Jensen eyed her and the others and then sighed loudly. He gave up his battle with Crouch and his grip of the gun.

"We solved nothing," he said wearily. "Nothing."

"You can recite that lament whilst you rot in jail."

"A lament? Yes, I have failed."

Alicia watched as Crouch moved back and Russo went over to help Healey and Caitlyn gain their feet. Both were bruised and sported small cuts but were otherwise okay.

She now saw the approach of local authorities, noticed the destroyed cathedral once more, and winced.

"Crap, this is gonna take some explaining."

Crouch shook his head. "That just won't work," he said. "We'd better start running."

## CHAPTER TWENTY EIGHT

Hours later, the running stopped.

Outside the new Panama City they found a refuge, a small clearing among the trees of a dense forest. Of course, Crouch could never go against the authorities; it would besmirch his reputation and endanger that which he loved the most—the treasure hunt—so he made sure to call people in authority that might be best placed to ease the team's way forward. The calls took time and then those people had to make more calls which also took time.

Hence, the team's decision to find a safe haven.

Alicia found herself wondering if it might be time to return to her primary team, and her new boyfriend, now that the bulk of the quest was out of the way. She felt a heap of disappointment, but also a little excitement at the thought of seeing Drake and the others again. She sat back on a blanket as Healey started a campfire and Russo took first watch. The night was black above, studded with twinkling pinpricks of light, and a thin sliver of moon barely crested the tops of the trees. A faint, fresh breeze played between the branches of trees and fanned the flames of their little fire.

Crouch finally returned from making his raft of calls.

"That's about all I can do," he said hopefully. "We have until morning."

Healey sat back and put an arm around Caitlyn. "For what? I mean, what's next? This is our third failure in a row."

"Look, cheer yourself up," Alicia said. "Take Caitlyn into the trees for ninety seconds or so. Come back with a smile on your face."

Healey ignored her, but sent a smile toward his girlfriend. Alicia thought she'd maybe lightened his mood and wondered if Russo might want a little company.

Then Crouch addressed the other member of their party. "So, Jensen? What happened to the final strongbox?"

The thin, dark-haired man held up his hands, rattling a pair of cuffs. "Take these off first."

Alicia chortled. "The stupidity is strong in this one."

"Do you know how many men you led to their deaths?" Crouch asked. "How much your little quest cost? How many ancient keepsakes you lost? You should take this chance to make some amends."

"It's still there," Jensen finally said. "Beneath the ruins. I have no use for baubles."

"Had," Alicia corrected. "You're all washed up, crazy man."

"It can't be over," Jensen rambled on. "It doesn't end this way. There has to be a treasure. Morgan wouldn't make all those damn maps for no reason."

"Where are the originals?" Crouch asked.

"Same place," Jensen said. "I left them in the car."

"And where is the base of *your* operations?"

"I won't tell you that. It has nothing to do with Henry Morgan. Does it not strike you as strange, Michael, that we have found not the barest hint of real treasure?"

It did. Alicia could see it in the boss's eyes. Crouch made a point of fixing a sandwich into Jensen's hands. The two men sat opposite and bolt upright, eyeing each other.

Alicia sensed trouble brewing. "What are you doing?"

"A little man to man," Crouch said. "That okay with you?"

"That'd take two men. Not a liar and a cheat."

Crouch looked hurt. Healey stared as if missing the point, which he did. Alicia waved it all away.

"Do what you must. I'll be out of here in the morning."

"We should talk first."

Alicia wrestled with it briefly. "Maybe." She wondered if she owed him at least that much.

Crouch then addressed Jensen. "In one aspect I do agree with you. There has to be a treasure. It's not at the bottom of the ocean unless it sank aboard one of the few ships of Morgan's that were never found, which I find a little coincidental. So where is it? Why draw these maps alluding to a large hoard if all he wanted to do was pinpoint the . . . baubles. It doesn't make sense."

"And the unquestionable fact is—there *was* a large hoard," Jensen said. "It's a documented history."

Alicia drifted somewhat as they talked back and forth. She tried to ignore the part where she thought Jensen acted an awful lot like Drake. She didn't agree with the polite questioning, or especially the humanization of Jensen, almost promoted to the level of equals, and found her mind wandering. It had been a little while since she took a look at the new self she was trying to embrace. Alicia of old was a tearaway, a sunset runner that never looked back and never cared much beyond the next dawn. If a problem arose she left it at her back, often crying for help. Then something—be it age or circumstance—had changed all that and made her realize that life could only be lived to the full by staying put, by confronting every challenge and rising above it. Part of that was why she had again agreed to help the Gold Team out; another part to find the answer to Beau's final riddle.

Had any of it helped?

She thought not. But it was good that she was still here and not a speck on the horizon. It was good that she had no desire to leave immediately. And it was especially good that she still felt willing to hear more of Crouch's explanation.

She zoned back in on the conversation.

Crouch had been flinging his maps to the ground. "Every last one a dead end. None interlinked. If you know something, Jensen, you'd best come clean now."

"You think I would be here, and at Viejo and all the others if I wasn't following the same fruitless trail as you?"

"So what's left?" Crouch conversed amiably with the criminal as they both sipped from bottles of water.

"Jail time," Alicia interjected harshly, purposely. "And plenty of it." She didn't want this thug to feel comfortable.

Jensen gave her a hard look. "This is Panama," he said.

Alicia frowned. What did he mean? She knew exactly where they were and the extent of American influence. Before she could question him further though, Crouch had again taken up the thread of their discussion.

"Morgan was a well-traveled man. Perhaps he ventured further afield."

Jensen stared at Alicia once more, and then at Crouch. His mind looked to be working overtime.

"If there's something you gotta say," Alicia said. "Do it now. 'Cause I can't promise I won't treat that mouth to a knuckle sandwich before bed."

Jensen understood the reference. "My situation," he said. "Is impossible. If I do help I won't get to see the outcome. Listen, have you really completed all your Henry Morgan research?"

Caitlyn sat up for that one. "Everything I could find on the Web. Why?"

"Well, there's a wealth of information not on the Web, Miss, I assure you. Only that which aggrandizes, embellishes or tarnishes is usually deemed worthy of repeating. Many a tome exists on the great captain, and only a few cover every single detail. *The Pirate King* and *Morgan, the Privateer Pirate's Treasure* are the best. Read them. I delve thoroughly into the background of my targets. We both do, right Michael? It's how we were trained."

"What is it that you have?" Crouch pushed.

"These books speak briefly of a stronghold that Morgan set up. Not a staging point, resting place or halfway stop for the pirates but a secure sanctuary he visited rarely and stayed at only briefly."

"You know of this stronghold but did not visit?" Crouch frowned.

"Not when we had the maps in our hands." Jensen shrugged. "Why would we?" He took a sip of water.

"All right," Caitlyn said. "Let's say you're telling the truth. Where is it?"

Jensen bit his lip. "Well, that I don't know. It's another reason I left it alone for what I thought was the easier option. The published books don't say where it is but . . ." he paused, thinking.

Crouch leaned forward. "What?"

"There's a maritime museum in Key West, some of which is devoted to Henry Morgan and his life and the stories that were written about him. Through research, through *books*," he shot a glance of disdain Caitlyn's way, "I learned that a first edition of *The Pirate King* is stored there and contains a later-removed, rather drab passage that describes exactly where the stronghold lies. I think that's our way to the treasure. At least, now I do."

Crouch considered it. "Even if you're telling the truth I'm not so sure," he muttered. "As you yourself said—the maps and this hunt had to have some kind of reason. Was it merely the baubles? Or something deeper?"

"Wait," Caitlyn said. "I can corroborate his claim. There should be a copy of *The Pirate King* online."

"And you're going to read it all now?" Jensen scoffed. "Spare me."

Caitlyn held up her cellphone and the screen showing a Word

app. "It's called technology," she said. "I can search for the word 'stronghold' and be taken to the right page in about, oh, half a second. But cheers for doing the grunt work."

Jensen grumbled. Alicia smiled at Caitlyn's effrontery. The girl was clearly annoyed with herself too. Within five minutes she had validated Jensen's claim.

"Well, the passage exists," she said. "But no mention of Key West. I checked the rest of the book."

"What makes you believe they have a first edition?" Crouch was looking tired now. Russo came out of the woods and Healey spotted him for a while. Jensen explained that they should check the museum's online records, and Caitlyn found that it did indeed list a first edition of *The Pirate King* among its own treasures.

"That's some clever research," Crouch told Jensen. "And thorough. A shame you couldn't bring yourself to put it to good use."

Alicia finished her meal. "I don't trust this ass one inch."

"Of course not," Crouch said. "But do we stay here and admit defeat . . ." He paused.

"Or do we go?" Caitlyn finished with a grin.

## CHAPTER TWENTY NINE

Key West sits at the southernmost tip of the Florida Keys, popular for its Duval Street attractions, its port and its blood-red sunsets. Alicia had initially felt gratified when Crouch called in the authorities and gave Jensen over to them; now as she walked the hot, tropical sidewalks of Key West, she found several moments of second-guessing. And when she voiced her concerns to Crouch the look he gave her only spoke to the fact that he shared her misgivings.

Still, the mission at hand was an attractive one. A quest that they had thought over still held promise. It wasn't unusual for newer versions of old tomes to be edited, cut down and repackaged. Publishers tried to make them more marketable, easier on the brain. Jensen had taken the time to research Henry Morgan to the full, but clearly hadn't trusted any one of his lieutenants enough to send them on this mission.

A small light bulb went off.

Where were his lieutenants?

They hadn't been present at the Viejo battle. Why not? Something more important was afoot. And Jensen himself had sent the Gold Team on this diversion. Still, they were here now and she wanted to see the outcome.

Time enough to worry later.

Tourists thronged the streets, aimlessly wandering between shops and bars, and trying to fit their cars into the tiny parking areas. Palm trees swayed happily in a light breeze. The smell of salt was in the air, tinged by diesel fumes. Colorful music spread from all corners and through shop doors, merging with the colorful locals and besotted tourists. The atmosphere galvanized a smile even from Russo.

"Feels like we should stay and play," he said in a rare moment of levity.

Alicia slapped his back. "There we go. I knew there was a party animal under that rough and ready exterior."

"Less animal." Russo had never been more flippant with her. "More warrior."

"The Party Warrior?" Alicia said. "You could probably market that."

Crouch led them down a side street and stopped in front of a pair of canons and a clean, tall gray building with lots of windows. Alicia remembered this place from a few years ago when she'd been flirting with the enemy. The memories weren't happy; the days since much better than those long past. She was thankful now for the change. She'd turned her life around and stuck with the motto: *One life, live it.*

We might all be dead tomorrow.

If she had learned one lesson, achieved one instant of enlightenment, that was it. They were living, they were there right now, so make the most of every moment in which you lived and loved and breathed.

Because death didn't care one bit. It didn't care who you left behind, who cried and who laughed, who missed you every single day. It didn't care who raised a glass or drove a mile or played a song for you. Alicia had stared death in the face a hundredfold, and told it to go fuck itself every time. She would do so again until that fateful moment finally came when she no longer wished to escape the cold embrace.

Crouch led the way up the steps and into the cool interior of the museum. In addition to its books it carried one of the largest collections of seventeenth-century shipwreck and pirate artifacts in the world. Just what they were looking for.

Crouch nodded in satisfaction as he read as much aloud.

"We came to the right place."

"Or were directed here," Alicia said.

"Don't be a pessimist. This is all part of the hunt. Be excited."

"Oh, I'm excited." Alicia sniffed as she looked around the well-presented and purposely shady interior. "Can't you tell?"

Artifacts gleamed from glass cabinets and low, polished pedestals. Maps and manuscripts glowed on the walls. Huge canons pointed the way to more impressive treasures. Crouch sought out the solitary guide among the numerous rooms and asked about the book they had come to see.

"Yes we have the book, *The Pirate King,*" the guide, a fifties-something woman with short hair and stern eyes, said. "But we don't generally lend it out. This is a museum, not a library, sir."

Crouch took the acerbity well. "But surely it is an artifact of sorts and could still prove useful. We could go straight to the right page. We'd wear gloves. You don't even have to move it."

"I don't know . . ."

"How about a donation?" Caitlyn asked. "Cash."

"You mean to the museum?"

Crouch shrugged indifferently. "We only need five minutes."

"I'll need to get back to the front."

They were taken through a high, dark opening into a small room where the walls were all glass cabinets and the spotlights shone down with bright abandon. Many volumes lay within the cabinets, all open and all covered in an ancient, spidery brown script. The guide led them straight to a corner, stopped in front of a chest-high row and produced a key. Alicia smelled polish in the air and some kind of cleaning chemical.

"Five minutes," the guide said. "Be cool. I'll be back."

Crouch opened the glass door and reached right in. Caitlyn had worked out the page number and location of the deleted passage, but hard reality was a little different to theory. It took

Crouch two minutes of squinting and careful flicking back and forth to find what they were looking for. Pages rustled and creaked rather alarmingly and he had to fight twice with the glass door which kept wanting to close. "Nothing worth doing," he said as he worked, "is ever easy."

"A guy told me that once," Alicia said with mock glumness. "Didn't know whether to thank him or hurt him."

"Does this sound right to you?" He stood back.

Caitlyn moved in. "I guess."

"You guess?"

Healey read the passage out: "And though he traveled often and tarried little, Henry Morgan did find himself a stronghold. Not a refuge but a fastness. It lay between Haiti and Panama and Port Royal, spoken of as a large mountain surrounded by a ribbon of beach with an unusual feature atop. A wizened, crooked, bent old tree, a hundred foot tall. A marker of passing time. No leaves, no branches, nothing but a stark, warped trunk. Why was it here? It was there to speak to the fanciful mind of the Pirate King.'"

"Interesting," Crouch said. "And yet I can see why they deleted it from the book. It really adds nothing of interest."

Alicia frowned. "To be fair—not even a location."

"Exactly. It's pretty vague in more ways than it's helpful. But . . ." Crouch turned with a smile. "A man of the seas, a sailor, a—"

"Pirate?" Caitlyn interrupted with a smile.

"Well, yes, whoever sails these Caribbean seas would know that island. All we have to do is find the right person."

"You're buying in?" Alicia asked.

Crouch grinned. "Who wouldn't?"

## CHAPTER THIRTY

John Jensen cooled his heels for several hours in a thirteen-by-thirteen jail cell. The mattress was narrow and hard, the pillow no better. The air conditioning was as cranky and ineffectual as a pensioner's complaint, the food bordering between slops and scraps. The police mostly ignored him, no doubt told there were bigger fish on the way to deal with the murderous criminal. He was looking at life. No parole. No sweet smelling lands for him anymore. No sweet tasting food nor women anymore.

Faced with the prospect of losing his freedom a man might be forgiven for a period of introspection. Brooding. Reflection on a life lived and opportunities missed. He might think hard about all the things that would continue as normal without him.

But not Jensen. A career soldier, he focused on the plan. A career criminal, he focused on the plan. Nothing wavered. Nothing changed. Grueling times often yielded lucrative results and this would be the best. Friends and lieutenants sometimes capitulated but Jensen simply left them behind. Some he even left breathing.

But still, time spent in a cell left even Jensen looking back. Where had the transition come between soldier and villain? He couldn't blame family or a poor upbringing. He couldn't blame a bad captain or vicious team. He was his own man. Always had been. The truth was—he enjoyed walking along the darker side of the thin line. It made him feel alive. A person existed only for a short span of time on this earth—his future was always diminishing. Jensen thought he might create his own legacy whilst he still lived.

Drifting from place to place, always moving, always savvy, he had sewn together a shabby band of mercenaries, added discipline and income and a little reward mixed with fear. An intelligent leader, he rarely put a foot wrong.

Is the risk worth the reward?

This time, damn right it was. Morgan's treasure was incalculable, and there were plenty of ruthless collectors out there that would pay twice as much as any government or museum. Jensen wished he knew the time. All he could see through his cell windows was a lessening of the light, so he knew evening was drawing in. All he could smell were microwave meals and his own stale sweat. Panama City was a great, steaming hive tonight, awash with misadventure and opportunity.

Tonight, he would carve out his own piece of history.

Jensen sat with his back to the wall, legs kicking gently. His heart beat rapidly. His mouth was dry so he took a drink from a plastic cup. At his back, the light faded away. If there had ever been a point of no return, Jensen knew this was it. His current crimes were serious but paled somewhat against what was soon to come.

*Not soon,* Jensen heard the beginning of it. *Now.*

They landed on the roof, and they would be led by Labadee, Forrester and Levy. Jensen had foreseen the need for more men, ever since he realized the final clue would not pan out, and had sent his three lieutenants on a search and recruit mission for reinforcements. For one last expedition in search of Morgan's treasure.

Panama was not without its corruptions. The right wallets had been filled to bursting; the correct leverages weighed. The doors he needed open would stay that way, at least for tonight.

The sound of gunfire, the shouting of men and women. An explosion. Some of it was set up by the men he'd paid off, but not all of it. This was how, occasionally, a rival was taken out of the picture or a debt settled. This was how a man with a shadow for a soul worked. Jensen worked hard to maintain his contacts. Ironically, it was a skill he'd learned from Michael Crouch.

Padding across the floor, he finished the last of his water and threw the plastic cup aside. A small rectangular hole gave him a glimpse into the corridor outside, but all he saw was a sink and a brown wall. Somewhere beyond, men yelled and screamed.

The sound of footsteps sent him retreating into his cell. After all, it could be anyone. The rattle of a bolt and then the door opened slowly. Labadee poked his head through.

"You ready?"

Jensen nodded at the Jamaican. "To get rich? Constantly."

"First, we must escape Panama." His lieutenant's voice was thick.

Jensen followed him out of the room and into the booking area. Cops stood around with their hands in the air, and one lay dead on the floor, bleeding out. Jensen gave none of them a second glance. The rear doors were open, leading straight out to an enclosed yard. Barbed wire topped the walls and CCTV cameras stood all around. Vehicles were parked or abandoned across the area. More bodies lay in between, some still groaning. Labadee pointed to the right where Jensen saw Forrester and Levy waiting. Both men scanned the surroundings and even as Jensen walked toward them Levy fired at a hidden cop, making him scurry for safety.

"Quickly," Forrester said.

"Our men?"

"Those not here are preparing the boat."

"Excellent."

Jensen longed for a drink; it was rare for a waking hour to pass when he didn't savor the rich nectar, his greatest companion. How could a man endure himself more than with such fine and luxurious help? Plus, it helped him think and kept all the ghosts at bay. Jensen believed that in keeping the ghosts of his past at bay he was in fact helping his fellow man, since accepting any of that amount of retribution would produce a terrible fallout. Maybe Henry Morgan should have drunk more.

Jensen wasn't about to part with any of his hard-earned currency. Not like Morgan. *Bury it nearby? Why? To give it back later?* Morgan never had. Jensen had read that Morgan started drinking himself to death as soon as he returned to Jamaica from his time in England.

Having gained a governorship, what then had he lost?

The guilt of all that plundering; the responsibility for so many innocent deaths. The remorse for a life ill-lived. Morgan had taken a different way out. He lost the will and the courage to be a survivor.

Jensen followed Labadee out of the station and toward the road. The assault had been direct and sudden. Merciless. Jensen approved. He had been taught by the other side long ago to strike hard and strike mean.

A sedan stood idling at the curb, its back door open and looking much more inviting than a jail cell. The road to the boat was a long one; the two wenches lounging along the back seat promising a distracting trip. Jensen waited as more shots rang out, preferring on this occasion not to join in with the bloodletting. There would be time enough for all that.

If Crouch found Morgan's abandoned island.

Jensen had gambled that to make time for himself and fashion a safe getaway, a true-enough tale had to be told. So he had given them the one about the abandoned island, the refuge

Morgan kept to himself; and the method in which Jensen himself had found it. Hopefully, the quest would keep them involved and Jensen would find the treasure and disappear before they figured it out.

Hopefully?

He was talking about Michael Crouch here. No way would he succeed in escaping before Crouch found the island.

So was it self-destruction? Did he want to be caught?

Or did he want to test himself against the best?

Jensen knew the answer without even thinking.

## CHAPTER THIRTY ONE

Alicia exited last from the museum, her senses alert even in the sleepy building. The bright sunlight blinded her for a moment, but then she was checking the streets outside and everything in the distance. Ironically, she remembered ambushing Matt Drake somewhere near here once, a fact she had long wanted to forget, and now looked to where she had positioned her own team during the Blood King conspiracy.

Key West bumbled along happily, bright, vivid and content in its relative seclusion at the southern tip of America. The only signs of life she could see were tourists, camera-snappers munching on the local and scrumptious item of fame—Key lime pie, and old locals sitting on metal benches, staring out to sea.

Crouch led the way to a taxi rank and the team decided to slip more comfortably into two separate cabs. The drivers agreed on a route that took them away from the busy Highway 1 and through Key West's residential suburbs, and pulled away from the curb. Alicia again assured herself that no one was following and that was when Crouch's cellphone rang.

She felt a small tingle, sensed trouble.

Crouch stared at the screen. "Unknown caller. Hello?"

He listened for a while, gripped the bridge of his nose, and scrunched his face up. "I see," he repeated four times and then ended with: "Any clue as to where?"

Alicia perceived that the answer was no and questioned the boss as he ended the call. "Didn't sound like a lottery win?"

"John Jensen escaped from prison," Crouch said with a pained exhalation. "Broke out by what they think was a ten-man team and a few insiders. There are casualties. Survivors gave chase but the man is gone."

Alicia closed her eyes in a moment of respect and then asked the obvious. "Where's he gone?"

"Wait." Crouch added Caitlyn and Healey, in the other car, to a conference call and quickly brought them up to speed.

"You think he's coming here?" Healey asked immediately. "To find the book?"

"It's possible," Crouch said.

Alicia saw him glance at the driver as if debating whether they should stay put. They were currently cruising past two rows of houses with palm trees waving in the gardens, white walls and white gates bordering the properties. Green refuse bins lined the sidewalks and cars were parked in haphazard fashion up and down the road. A woman dragged a shopping trolley on wheels across a junction ahead, slowing the cabs, and a man worked under the raised hood of an old Buick. A lethargic air hung over the city as it waited for the sun to begin its descent into the west.

"We can check for movements," Crouch said, "aliases. But remember, Jensen sees himself as a pirate captain. Wouldn't he escape using the sea?"

Alicia shrugged. "You can't count on a madman acting predictably."

"Good point," Russo said from the front seat. "We could spin around and put a watch on the museum."

"How many ways could he get in?" Alicia wondered.

"Normal routes," Crouch said. "Smugglers' routes. We can't watch them all."

"But wait," Caitlyn's low voice stopped their speculations in their tracks, "there is another possibility."

Crouch nodded. "Yes, I know."

"Anyone care to inform us?" Russo asked.

Caitlyn was already speaking. "Jensen already knows where the island is," she said. "And sent us off with an authentic clue to get us out of the way. Remember, he actually did my research for me."

"Knowing," Crouch added, "that we would eventually find the location and head straight for the island. It's a tactic I should have foreseen."

"Where he'll be waiting?" Alicia asked, a tad hopefully.

"Either that, or long gone. Pawing through his ill-gotten gains."

The team reflected for a few minutes before Crouch made the decision. "We'll inform the local cops," he said. "Put them on the museum and the access routes. We need to find that island."

"Not to mention the treasure," Russo said.

"No." Alicia glanced at their driver. "You're right. Only a knob-end would mention that."

"But where to now?" Healey asked. "Back to Panama? Jamaica?"

"Our goal remains the same," Crouch said. "We find a man that knows that island. The passage said look between Haiti, Panama and Port Royal. I think Jamaica would be the perfect place to ask around."

Alicia thought the plan had merit. Judging by the satnav, they were starting to get close to the airport now, though it was screened behind a row of houses and tall trees to their right. They passed a driveway inhabited only by a speedboat, and a white house built on stilts so a fleet of cars could be parked easily in the shade underneath.

Ahead a black SUV approached.

Alicia squinted toward the blacked-out interior. "You see that?"

Crouch spoke into the cellphone. "Healey? How are we back there?"

"Black SUV just pulled out of a side street. Approaching fast."

"Shit."

Alicia told the driver to put his foot down just as the man started to slow. The SUV swerved into their path. Russo leaned over and wrenched the wheel out of his hands. "Get down."

"How did they find us?" Caitlyn asked.

"Easy," Crouch breathed. "*They* were watching the bloody museum."

"That's some forward planning on Jensen's part."

"Well, like it or not, the guy's good. Or at least, he was. You don't lose that kind of training."

Russo turned the wheel so that their vehicle bounced up onto the narrow, barren patch of earth that ran parallel to the sidewalk. Rutted, it played havoc with their tires, sending Alicia slamming into the doorframe and Crouch against the back seat.

"C'mon, Robster. You ever drive before?"

"Not with my head in this guy's lap. You wanna jump over and try it yourself, be my guest."

"Oh, you'd like that wouldn't you?" Alicia managed to find her gun as the SUV slammed by to their left, sideview mirrors crashing together and shearing away. The smoked-glass windows in the other car remained closed, adding to the mystery as it slewed around in the road just behind Healey and Caitlyn's cab. Dust plumed up into the air and tires squealed. Onlookers jumped back into their gardens.

"Slam the accelerator!" Russo shouted at the driver to a look of utter confusion.

"The gas," Crouch said. "Hit the bloody gas."

The car lurched ahead, sending out a smoke-plume of its own. The SUVs were more powerful, though, and were soon all over the back ends of their quarries. Alicia looked back and knew they had a matter of seconds.

"Faster."

They switched roads, still running parallel to the airport. The maneuver opened up a small gap but not enough. Alicia opened her window and leaned out, gun ready.

"Stick your head out now," she murmured to herself. "See where it ends up."

The SUVs windows powered down in sync. Arms holding machine pistols emerged and, rather than ducking back, Alicia took potshots at them. Russo swerved the cab at every opportunity and Crouch twisted his body so he could lean out of the other window. At first only Alicia's gunshots filled the air, but then fire was returned and the deadly sound of automatic gunfire shuddered around them. Alicia saw metal flatten and almost instantly the back window shattered. Now she ducked, feeling the impact as more bullets thudded into the car's chassis to left and right and through the trunk.

Russo manhandled the cringing driver out of the way, depositing him into the footwell of the passenger seat. Once behind the wheel he shifted it better, zigzagging for their lives and hitting one large red trashcan so that it spun into the car behind. The tree-lined road stretched on. Alicia fired blindly through the rear window. Crouch popped his head up.

"To the left a little," he said. "Perfect."

Alicia glanced through the broken glass to see the pursuing vehicle's windshield destroyed and two men wearing sunglasses revealed. The driver leaned away from the center, probably thinking the frame might give him shelter. Alicia knew he was their best chance. Before she could fire he rammed his own gas pedal to the floor and screamed at his companion to shoot. Bullets riddled the cab. Russo turned sharply again and again. Then he stepped hard on the brake pedal and the other car crashed right into their rear fender.

Alicia's eyes widened in surprise as she saw the passenger fly through the air, land on their own trunk, and grip hold of the razor-edged glass that remained in the rear window, desperate to hang on.

Alicia rose.

Staying beneath the man's head for shelter, she lunged at him. Her fist connected hard with his forehead, causing a splutter and a scream of pain. Still he hung on, twisting with the car's momentum and ignoring the blood that seeped between his fingers. The spare hand, held down at his side, still gripped the gun and he brought it around now to aim at Alicia. She saw it coming—the arc of the arm and the effort required was substantial—and she leaped up to catch it. Now face to face with the man, swinging from side to side and buffeted by sudden gusts of wind, she struggled hard.

She slammed her forehead into the bridge of his nose, sending blood trickling into his eyes. She forced the gun hand as far away as she could. A bullet ripped from the barrel, burying itself into the road. He tried to headbutt her back, but Alicia had been wise to that move since high school, and dipped her skull. She let go of the rear window frame with her right hand and punched him in the cheek. Dynamite went off behind his eyes; she felt she saw it clearly. She punched again and he was out cold, gone, tumbling off the rear end and spinning away. Now the driver was vulnerable.

Crouch had already lined him up. The men in the back seat pushed their weapons forward through the gap but Crouch fired first, a perfect shot through the center of the driver's skull. The black SUV swerved and crashed, tipping onto its side, another man thrown clear.

Alicia saw the second attacker now as it hounded Healey's cab.

The young soldier's driver was nowhere to be seen. Caitlyn sat behind the wheel, trying to block the following car and stop it from coming up alongside. The researcher's reactions were slow and only Healey's careful shooting was keeping them from being stopped. Alicia knew they had to come up with a fast plan.

"Russo. Three sixty and brake in ten seconds. Crouch—you still on that open line?"

"I am."

"Tell Caitlyn to hold steady and hope she hears."

Crouch complied and readied himself as Alicia counted the seconds down for Russo. On cue the big man stamped on the brakes and threw the cab into a three-hundred-and-sixty-degree turn, ending up with the nose pointing toward the two oncoming vehicles. Alicia and Crouch emptied their clips at the SUV as Caitlyn powered by on the left so close they lost another sideview mirror.

Bullets ripped apart the SUV, fragmenting the windshield and both men in the front seat. Traction was lost and the vehicle spun badly, ending up on its side. A man pushed himself up through a rear door and Alicia picked him off with ease, watched him slump still with his rear body in the SUV. Crouch told Russo to make a fast getaway.

"Move it, before any more turn up."

"We Jamaica bound?" Russo asked as he helped the panic-stricken driver up into a proper seated position.

Crouch punched in another number that would connect him to the police. "Oh, yeah, as soon as we get this particular shitstorm sorted out."

"And meanwhile Jensen gets closer and closer to the treasure," Alicia said.

"Oh, don't worry," Crouch assured her. "We're not out of this hunt yet."

## CHAPTER THIRTY TWO

Jamaica, and in particular Port Royal, offered up a whole host of possibilities. The tricky part was plucking the genuine probability from the raft of chance that was offered. Many men knew the location of the mountain-like island with the barren tree on top. Of course they did. And they all wanted cash up front.

In the end, Crouch sought the help of his Jamaican contact and the team were directed to a Jamaican roadside bar; a ramshackle beat-up place the size of a market stall and with the only signage being a large white plaque out front that read: *Cold Beer Joint.* Plastic chairs and tables stood around and a tall man with thick hair leaned over the counter, staring at their approach with lazy eyes.

"Help you folk?"

Crouch nodded. "We're looking for Ric?"

"You found him, folks. What's up? Nice cool beer?"

Alicia found herself licking her lips. "I'd sure love one."

Ric cracked open beers as Crouch talked to him.

"Heard you were a fisherman back in the day. Some kind of sailor too." The boss described the island they were looking for as Alicia drank deeply, savoring the taste. "We were hoping you might be able to take us there?"

Ric pursed his lips and laughed. "Oh, man, I am going nowhere. My sailing days are long gone. I know the place you mean, but I won't be leaving this shore again."

"We have much to offer." Crouch made the universal money sign.

"Don't care if you're offerin' me Shakira in a Lamborghini. I ain't takin'."

Alicia paused with her lips around the mouth of the bottle. "Really? I might."

Ric made a shooing gesture. "Have at it."

Crouch looked despondent. "Is there anything we could offer you?"

"Got all I need right here in this shack, man. Do I look unhappy to you?"

Crouch admitted that he didn't.

"Had my fair share of material shit. Had money. Had women. It's all jus' complication. Out here—" he spread his arms "—is easy. Out here—you live long and happy."

"And lonely," Alicia pointed out, still drinking. "I know about running. Truth is, it gets you nowhere."

"Who says I'm running?"

"Well, my contact actually." Crouch smiled. "Says you owe a tidy sum in back taxes."

"Shit."

"But we're not here to hassle you. We just need a little help."

"Shit."

"Either way, we never saw you."

"Duppy Island, you say?"

"Is that what it's called? We can't find it on any map."

"Nah. Nobody go there. Only a Yardie knows."

"A Yardie?"

"A local. Jamaican. And a duppy is a ghost. Duppy Island be crawling with 'em."

"Shit." Now it was Alicia's turn to curse.

"You believe inna duppy?"

"'Course not. What kind of ghosts?"

Ric shrugged. "Lotta dead there through the years. Pirates mostly." He looked away. "Don't want talk 'bout it."

"If you won't take us there, can you show us where it is?" Crouch pointed toward Caitlyn's laptop. "Exactly?" Their contact had explained that Ric had once been a competent showboat captain and an explorer of the local area. He would have a wide knowledge of all things nautical.

"You mean real coordinates? Nah. But I can sail you close if you got a real good digital map."

Caitlyn placed her laptop on one of the plastic table tops. "Ready to go."

Ric slowly unstuck his body from the counter as Caitlyn raised the screen, then came around using a languid gait. For a man essentially on the run, Alicia had never seen anyone so laid-back.

"I guess police chases happen around here on a whole different level," she remarked.

Ric ignored her and peered at the screen. Pinpointing Port Royal, he took a virtual voyage first toward Haiti and then Panama, east then south across the Caribbean Sea, zooming in at points of interest—sandbars, reefs and unnamed islands too small to be of any interest—before sailing on. When he found a spit of land shaped like a spoon he grumbled, adjusted his positioning and started afresh from there. Half an hour passed as Ric ran a painstaking eye over their journey. At last he pointed at what could only be described as the tiniest ring of land amid the sea.

"That is Duppy. Be careful there. It is . . . overrun."

Crouch nodded happily. "By ghosts, yes. Thank you so much, Ric." He pumped the Jamaican's hand and turned to the others with a huge smile on his face.

"We have it."

Alicia grunted. "Let's hope, this time, it's not a local's wristwatch."

"Have faith. On Duppy, there are no locals."

"Don't forget the ghosts."

Russo ran a hand over the back of Alicia's neck, making her shiver. "You scared, sweetie?"

Alicia grabbed the hand and bent the fingers until their owner pleaded for mercy. "Sweetie?"

"I meant *bitch*. Sorry, sorry I really meant bitch."

"That's better." Alicia let him go.

"If you two are ready," Crouch started walking back toward their vehicle, "it's time to set sail in search of the treasure."

Alicia followed with Russo. "How the hell did he say that without using a pirate accent? I know I couldn't."

"I guess he's a pro."

"Aw, sore that I bent your likkle fingers?"

"Barely felt a thing. The noises were to help you feel better."

Alicia slapped the man on the shoulders as they neared the car. Behind them, Healey and Caitlyn walked so close no daylight passed between them. The final hunt was on, and the team were ready.

"Let's hope we're not walking into a trap," Alicia said, climbing in. "Or into hell on earth."

"Shit," Russo said. "Now you've gone and bloody jinxed it."

## CHAPTER THIRTY THREE

The team planned their boat trip so that they neared the island as darkness descended in its entirety. Using their benefactor's wealth and influence they had managed to rent a large, sleek, ocean-going yacht from Port Royal and programmed their coordinates into the advanced auto-pilot system. Sometimes it paid to be acting for well-off individuals known for their entrepreneurship and contributions to local governments. A man that could open the doors of power with a single phone call.

Michael Crouch found it increasingly hard to suppress the excitement as he neared what he believed would prove to be yet another historic achievement. Men had searched for Henry Morgan's long lost treasure through the centuries, through long years lost in the mists of time; men long dead and turned to dust themselves. And none had prevailed. Crouch lived for the hunt.

Which was nearing its end.

All the years of living for the job, of training soldiers and planning missions. All the times he'd coached and planted men like Beau to go behind enemy lines, to become part of a terrible organization. Some of those decisions haunted him now. All had seemed necessary at the time.

But time itself lent a new perspective to "necessary."

Everything changed. Even me. Even correct decisions. Even concrete chipped and eroded and faded away. We can only do what we think is morally right.

The boat began to slow and, on the digitized display before

them, the team saw the details of the approaching island. Assuming they would be here well past sunup they anchored the large yacht well offshore and broke out the motorized dinghies.

Caitlyn transferred the map's specifications from the on-board computer to her smartphone. The island wasn't large but it would still be good to be able to find their way around and know the location of coves, beaches and places of sanctuary. Assuming Jensen would have landed at the most easily accessible cove, they plotted a course to one of the hardest and set out in two dinghies, wearing black and carrying loaded weapons, invisible in the darkest part of the night.

The sea buffeted them gently, soft swells passing by. The moon presented a thin sliver of silver that bounced across the waves and offered the barest amount of light to see by. Crouch took what he could get, embracing the dark and using the faint illumination to navigate closer to a beach bounded by rocky outcroppings. They were jarred, tipped left and right, glanced once and then twice off the thin tips of rocks, dinghies shaken but remaining intact, bounced between swells, and skipped off the top of a curling wave. They were left rousted, but safe as they finally drifted up to shore, the shifting waters giving way to a soft beach, silver in the quarter-light and happily empty.

Crouch had always been confident about their landing point. It was where they went afterward that might prove difficult. A proper recce was called for, as they needed to know enemy positions, numbers and extent of firepower in short order.

No sign of Jensen then.

Crouch walked carefully along the beach as Alicia and Russo found a safe place for the dinghies. Soon, he was standing before the tree line, peering into a darker interior. As his eyes adjusted, something began to take shape.

Something that flickered.

"What *is* that?" he whispered, a breath no louder than silk on a breeze.

"Is it a ghost?" Alicia peered hard.

Crouch parted a lattice of branches. "Oh, hell. I never expected that. Oh no."

Alicia took a step back in surprise. "Am I seeing things, or is that—"

"It is," Crouch said, still staring. "It is."

Flickering for as far as the eye could see were dozens and dozens, possibly hundreds, of virtually smokeless campfires. They were all under the dense tree line, and the trees ran more than halfway up the grassy hill that formed the bulk of the island; their lurid flames painting the sides of tents crimson, the trees with blood, and large pavilions with their big stretched canvases in orange. Flames sputtered everywhere, attesting to the presence of a large group of men.

Crouch backed away very carefully. Close to the lapping waves he gathered the team around. "I don't know what to think. Surely Jensen can't have gathered so large a force."

Alicia shifted. "We can always take a closer look."

"Go among them? Do you think you can pull it off? One bad move and all hell would be unleashed. I think we're talking over a hundred men out there."

"I could do it," Alicia said. "Alone. No Sasquatch or inseparable twins beside me."

They all glared, but said nothing. The truth was, Alicia was right and Crouch and the others all knew it. Crouch sent a glance toward the top of the large hill, the center of the island, which nobody could see from here.

"I'm wondering what is going on. In my experience a large crew like this means an awful lot more than a random treasure hunt. I hope we anchored the boat far enough offshore."

"We did," Caitlyn assured him. "Unless they sail that way."

Crouch nodded silently, wondering too about the fate of Jensen. Was the ex-SAS madman already here? Surely this force wasn't his. Crouch had to believe that Jensen was in hiding somewhere, pondering options.

"Alicia can do it," he said unnecessarily. "And we need the Intel. I have to say though—it's a dangerous, lethal mission. If you're noticed, you won't get out of there alive and we're unlikely to be able to come in after you." He shook his head. "It's suicide."

Alicia laughed. "Seriously? It's any day of the week, then. I'll see you soon, guys. Don't wait up."

She turned away.

Crouch watched her walk into the lion's den, remembering the years and the missions and finding it hard to think of a person he admired or cared for more. The worst of it was—he had let her down. The explanation was hard, and clear, but hardly flattering. Leaders were often forced to make the difficult decisions, ones they later may have made differently, and Beau's inside Intel had paid off at least half a dozen times, foiling entire plots.

Still, Alicia had suffered and Crouch hated himself for it. He spoke to her retreating back as she walked away.

"Be safe."

She never heard it. Or maybe she chose to ignore it. Either way, the message was the same.

## CHAPTER THIRTY FOUR

Flames flickered and spat at the darkness; lurid, dancing light in one place revealing the dangers, deep playful shadow in the other, concealing them. Campfires stretched across an area hundreds of feet wide and on up the steady slope of the huge hill at the end. Tents stood around the fires, some dangerously and uncaringly close to the flames. Pavilions stood dotted and tied between trees. Alicia knew this was a permanent camp, a home of sorts. But the identity of those that lived here so far remained a mystery.

Without a sound she advanced to within throwing distance of the perimeter, taking time to pause, listen and become attuned to the camp's general ambiance. The faint music. The raucous laughter. Other sounds came from behind canvas. Chiefly, she looked for guards and wanderers, those that might stumble upon her. Of the latter there were a few, but of the former there were none. At least, not so close to the camp.

Perhaps they were positioned nearer the shore. After all, the only danger to these people would come from the seas.

Alicia stood with her back pressed up against a tree, blending with the dark and the leafery as best she could. Her eyes swept the camp, flicked off every pit of fire and noted every loose piece of canvas. A man with long, matted hair and a bare chest staggered between rows, belched and then disappeared into a tent. Another came out for a fast smoke before discarding the remnants into a fire and ducking back inside his makeshift home once again.

This man carried an old-style machine gun. The barrel

dangled at his side, pointing at the ground.

Alicia thought she might know what kind of men these were. And the knowledge was incredibly ironic.

She felt she'd adapted to her environment enough, and stepped out into the camp.

Wearing black, wandering from point to point, blending as well as she was able, Alicia walked the campfire gauntlet. A dark sky looked down upon her, interspersed by drifting clouds tinged around the edges by the silver moon. Branches crackled underfoot, but that was fine because they crackled and spat in every small fire. The first obstacle she encountered in her path was a large, prone figure, snoring loudly. Passed out from the liquor, he held a machine gun in one hand and a bottle of vodka in the other. His face was dirty, his clothes old and tattered. Almost like his features, which Alicia guessed were old before their time. Seen too much and done too much. There was no redemption for men like these.

Picking her way past the figure, she moved on. Heat from a campfire washed her face from the right. A movement against a tent wall to the left sent her to the floor, waiting patiently. It appeared to be a man falling over. She waited a minute for the snoring to start and then rose carefully and crept on. The tents themselves afforded some cover, but the dancing fires sent her shadow flitting in all directions.

Past the tent she moved to another and another, listening hard at every step and keeping a careful eye to every perimeter. At first she worried that a woman's figure might single her out in the camp, but she soon saw other females that were part of the crew, wandering between tents, armed to the teeth. No figures hung around the edges of the camp and she had to assume it wasn't closely guarded. Deductions? These people had been here a while, saw no obvious danger to their settlement, and didn't particularly care what happened during the night. They were too comatose to notice, no doubt just like Henry Morgan's men hundreds of years before them.

Still evaluating and listening, Alicia pressed deeper into the camp. A tent flap rattled near her left knee but nobody emerged. The sound of a rifle cocking behind her made her spin, weapon ready, but all was clear. Another undercover episode. Still composed, she picked her way among the flames.

A head popped out of a tent opening to her right.

"Hey girl, where you goin'?"

Alicia thought: *Girl? Really?* but moved and leaned in close to the filthy individual that had spotted her. "You alone in there?"

"Oh yeah, for now."

Her face hovered before his, sending an unwashed stench into her nostrils. "So what are you waiting for?"

The man backed away inside his tent, double-time, and Alicia followed. It was a small space, taken up by a hard mattress and a backpack. Two rifles leaned against the back canvas.

"Mattress?" the man asked. "Or floor?"

Alicia glared. "Oh, you're such a charmer."

"Been said before, girl. By man and woman." The man was already unzipping.

"Oh, you swing that breadstick both ways, do ya?"

"Huh?" The man looked down. "Well, in this camp you have to."

"As attractive as you make all that sound." Alicia came close. "I have to reject you."

"Wha—"

He collapsed without making any noise, unconscious, bruised around the temple. Alicia tied and gagged him, but couldn't bring herself to help the zipper situation so just left everything hanging out. He'd probably never notice. She slipped her head back out of the tent, saw all was still clear, and resumed her mission.

Then Crouch was in her ear. "We found a guard out by the beach. Drunk and unconscious. We think there's another around the other side, but don't want to get close. Keep seeing the end of a burning cigarette and hearing the sound of a bottle clunking."

Alicia tapped twice to show she had heard, but didn't reply. The guards—if they could be called that—watched the sea then. Of course they appeared to have been located here for years, so complacency was a given, especially considering the amount of alcohol and drugs she'd already seen about the place.

Someone was going to regret it in the morning.

Still, their numbers were large enough to be worrying. And what had happened to Jensen? Alicia thought she knew. If the self-acclaimed pirate boss had known about this place, he'd have also surely known about the force that occupied it. Clearly, he'd chosen a safe route and was probably ensconced inside some rum-sodden hidey hole.

Waiting for... what?

She delved further into the camp, halfway through now and well past the point of no return. The fires still burned strong; men tended them every now and again. To them she was a shadow, barely discernible. She froze in her tracks as two men exited a tent and sauntered by, cursing and laughing at some uproarious joke. They passed her position only a meter away, not noticing the crouching blonde at the side of the nearest tent. On one of the men's belts swung a set of handcuffs, on the other a huge hunting knife and a coiled rope. Curious. She held her breath as their boots tramped the grass before her, then stopped, the men spotting something after all.

"What da fuck is dat?"

"Jus' Jeff, man. He up dat tree."

"Ya mon. I see now."

Alicia slowly turned her head so she could see what they were seeing. Beyond their waists she saw a thick oak bordering the camp and a figure sitting with his legs on either side of a wide branch. The harness that kept him up there stretched taut as he had clearly fallen off whilst fast asleep. Both men stared.

"Y'think we should help?"

"Naa, mon. Dis is cool. He drinkin' too much bag juice."

Both men guffawed, then moved off. Alicia let out a deep breath. If the quest for Morgan's treasure had been fraught with nothing but bad luck so far, tonight had gone a little way to evening the score. She waited until the camp quieted again before moving to an area near the back, where the slope of the hill began. Here a row of tents had been lashed together, and a perimeter fence staked down at chest height. Whoever inhabited those tents would not easily leave.

Prisoners.

Alicia was sure now. These men—this band of callous, neglectful, dirty, well-armed thugs—were nothing but modern day pirates. Men that roamed the seas looking for boats and people to kidnap and ransom. Men that lived to steal and hurt and terrify. These kind of pirates smuggled people, belongings and even bodies through borders and across the waves, meeting the demands of ruthless entities such as terrorist organizations and the worst criminal enterprises. Alicia knew they brought the word pitiless down to a whole new level. For most of them, life had not been easy and they had no clue how real people and the real world actually worked. They made rich men richer, and took everything they wanted.

Alicia saw some of the signs of their occupation smoldering away in a fire in front of the row of tents. Piles of clothes, burned and still smoking. Whoever had once worn those clothes clearly no longer had a use for them.

Alicia paused before the fence, well aware of her exposure

but feeling a pull toward what could well be an imprisoned family. The area also appeared unguarded and a close check of trees and nearby tents revealed no sentries. Alicia moved to the rough gate and looked at the lock.

A length of twine, knotted around. Classy.

With nowhere to hide, she turned and surveyed the camp. Very little moved out there save for the flickering of flames. Another man emerged from another tent, making her drop low, but he soon vanished without even looking around. Tension caused the muscles across her shoulders to knot but she shrugged it off. Even a seasoned soldier found it hard to deal with such relentless danger and having to keep a hyper-awareness. A guard now exited a nearby tent and looked over at her. Alicia sauntered away, conscious his eyes never left her back.

It didn't look right. She was going to be exposed.

"You want something?" His voice echoed.

Alicia held up a hand and chose a tent at random, conscious that she wore no metal-plated vest or other protection in her efforts to blend. To look back would only increase his mistrust so she fell to her knees and pushed at a tent flap. The material gave and she climbed in.

Face to face with two bearded men.

Both stared at her with wide eyes, mouths working but making no sound. Both were bare chested and hairy. They played cards, drank alcohol and chewed on some kind of blackened meat. And, perhaps trusting some kind of brutish sixth sense, they both reached for their weapons.

Alicia acted instantly, knowing there was no going back now. She launched herself at the men, but not in a panic-stricken way. She attacked with precision, using the lessons learned from hundreds of face-to-face battles. The man to the left was quickest, fingers already brushing the barrel of his Uzi, but it was pointed the wrong way and tangled with a bed sheet. So she swooped for the other, clamping his wrist before he managed to even touch the cool metal, twisting and breaking bone just as she clamped a hand over his mouth.

The scream went unheard.

Wrenching again, she twisted his arm until his face showed he was too concerned about the pain than the screaming, and she left him collapsed on his knees. Now she switched to the other man who was just bringing his own Uzi to bear. Alicia let it come around, knowing he would be fully concentrated on the weapon and its deadly uses, which was his weakness.

The barrel brushed her forehead.

She brought the hilt of her knife up under his chin, through the roof of his mouth and on, watched his eyes bulge and felt the machine gun fall between her knees.

Twisting again, she didn't let up. Her first opponent was finding an extra burst of adrenalin as he saw his comrade die. But still, like almost everyone that hadn't been trained, he focused on the one thing he thought gave him the advantage—the gun. Alicia watched him reach out, bend slightly, waiting for the precise moment, then used his own lunge to turn him around and put a chokehold around his throat.

No sound. No warning cries. Just the dying chokes of a ruthless modern-day pirate.

She ended it faster with the knife, then let him fall gently to the floor of the tent. She looked around, wondering now that she had a tent to herself if there was anything of importance she might find. With low-level crooks such as these she suspected to find nothing, but would look anyway.

Underneath the bunk was a pile of magazines and spare clothes. The low picnic table in the corner—the owner's only furnishing—held an assortment of what appeared to be trophies. A gold watch, a pearl bracelet, a pair of cufflinks.

Alicia bit her bottom lip as she stared at possessions that had once belonged to innocent people, no doubt captured by this band of callous mercenaries and ransomed or tortured and killed. She looked over at the dead, bleeding bodies and felt no remorse, only a pang of distress at the knowledge that they had once been as innocent and young and carefree as any child born anywhere. Somebody had made them this way. Somebody made a deliberate decision to make a child become . . . this.

She turned away, taking a moment to regain focus. She needed every ounce of concentration now.

Footsteps stopped right outside the tent.

## CHAPTER THIRTY FIVE

"Hey mon, all good in der?"

The thick tones were so close to her ear Alicia thought for a moment the man had stuck his head through the loose flap. She realized he was bending down, listening. She looked around at the dead men, the seeping blood. Probably not what the new pirate wanted to see.

She hated herself in one way but knew the old Alicia wouldn't mind doing what she did next.

"Ahh," she whispered softly. "Yeah, that's it. Right there."

She moaned softly.

"Jake? That you?"

Stifling a retort, she played it out a bit further and a bit louder. "All the way in. Go on . . . just . . . oh, yeah."

Silence for five seconds made Alicia let out another series of sounds. A shuffling of feet tensed her body and made her ready the knife.

"All right, mon. You be happy." Footsteps moved away, vanishing into the night.

Alicia gave it five minutes and then carefully pushed her head through a gap in the bottom of the tent. Darkness and stillness presented in equal measure, so she squeezed through and back outside. The camp looked the same as she reacquainted herself, then took a few minutes to look beyond the prison tents and on up the steady slope to the top of the hill. It was a busy stretch of land up there—not only dotted with campfires and tents but also crowded with thick brush and undergrowth, trees and outcroppings, natural curved features and random boulders. On the plus side it offered quite a bit of cover; on the downside it would be hard to negotiate properly. Danger lived in that climb, danger as lethal as any she'd ever known.

Taking care, she skirted the hill as best she could, seeing no alternatives, and then started to make her way back through the camp. She fancied she could see an early smudge of dawn marking the lowest horizon. She wondered how she'd managed to stay in there half the night. No further communications had come from Crouch, but that was as it should be. The team wouldn't want to compromise her. A double-click every half hour told them she was staying out of trouble.

As much as Alicia Myles was able.

As she neared the edge of the camp she began to hear the muted sounds of men waking, the coughing and the yawning. She guessed the sentries would be on their way back in. Creeping low, she heard a sound in the undergrowth outside the camp and froze. Waiting, she saw Russo.

"Hey." Her voice was pitched low. "Hey. Here."

Russo looked over, saw her move, and hunkered down at her side.

"What the hell are you doing here?"

"Looking for you. We thought..."

Alicia shushed him with a finger to his lips as another creaking and crashing sound attested to the presence of another individual—this one clearly born without any realization of the word stealth. One of the guards, looking sleepy and hungover, barged through, snagging his clothes on branches and scratching bare skin, not caring. Alicia stared at Russo as the man passed them by, four feet away but oblivious. When he was gone Russo prized the finger from his lips.

"Don't ever do that again. I have no idea where that finger of yours has been."

"Oh, I think you do, Rob," Alicia whispered cheekily. "I really think you do."

Together, they made their way back to Crouch and the others. The boss had found a nice hiding place, an eroded overhang surrounded by rocks and whispering waves on three sides, a mini-cave with its rocky back to the island. Alicia picked her way over the rocks to the dry back part of their hiding place.

Crouch nodded. "Report?"

Alicia laid it all out, from the state of the camp and the men in the tents to the hazardous hill and the prisoner area and the ancient weapons. She voiced her opinion that this group was a band of modern-day pirates.

"Worst of the worst," Russo grunted. "Scavengers. They care little about life."

"They are likely to find the ones I killed," Alicia said.

"I guess it happens most nights," Russo said. "I doubt they'll care, except for those chosen to take care of the burial."

"Any sign of who's in charge?" Crouch asked the question a leader would wonder about.

"Nothing. No special tents, no banners or black flags."

"It's not a joke. We could use the info."

"I know. It's the whole pirate angle is getting to me. No sign of Captain Flint, sir."

Crouch sat back on his heels, spine against the rock. "Then what next? Where's Jensen going?"

"I find it hard to believe you guys haven't figured that out by now. What have you been doing all night?" Alicia looked suspiciously from face to face.

"First, we searched for guards. Then Jensen. Then we got some kip," Russo said. "Thought you'd be back hours ago."

"Oh, so you were all just sleeping whilst I tussled with two men in a tent?"

They all stared, not quite sure what to say. Healey broke the silence. "Is that a movie title, or real life?"

Alicia sighed. "I give in."

Caitlyn came to her rescue, reciting the passage they already knew. "And though he traveled often and tarried little, Henry Morgan did find himself a stronghold. Not a refuge but a fastness. It lay between Haiti and Panama and Port Royal, spoken of as a large mountain surrounded by a ribbon of beach with an unusual feature atop. A wizened, crooked, bent old tree, a hundred foot tall. A marker of passing time. No leaves, no branches, nothing but a stark, warped trunk. Why was it here? It was there to speak to the fanciful mind of the Pirate King."

"We already know all that."

"Yes, and we think it also points to what the author believed was the place where Morgan buried the bulk of his treasure. Where else? It says 'marker'. It says 'speak to the fanciful mind of the Pirate King', meaning he would find significance by using such a clear marker in the middle of so large a sea. Morgan would see it as a sign. He made this place his stronghold, after all. Total security for as long as he pirated the Caribbean seas. A visit every few months to drop the wealth off. It's a very strong pointer."

"You think the treasure is buried beneath the twisted, barren tree?"

"At the top of the mountain."

"Hill."

"Not in the fanciful tales." Caitlyn laughed. "It's always a mountain, Alicia. Always."

Alicia plonked herself atop a boulder. "Well, I'm sorry to be the bearer of bad news, guys. But that *mountain* is gonna be an utter bitch to climb, nigh on impossible. It's hard-going, half-full of tents and fires, littered with brush, trees and rocks. You won't do it in daylight, and at night," she spread her arms, "bones are the least you'd be breaking. Skulls most likely; one slip and you'll roll down to your death, or imprisonment, and then we'd all be outed. Trapped behind the enemy camp with nowhere to go. It's a logistical nightmare."

"Do I hear Alicia Myles being cautious?" Russo mock-gasped. "Shit, did the tent tussle cure you?"

"You hear a soldier telling you the lay of the land, and you'd best listen. Seriously, I'm up for anything but we're going on supposition here. A passage in a book that could also mean something else entirely."

"It doesn't," Caitlyn said. "This time—it's real. And Jensen wouldn't have come if he didn't believe it too."

"Maybe." Alicia forced them to listen to the single word. "Maybe."

"How many pirates?" Crouch asked.

"Around seventy. Could be a hundred."

"We would have to go tonight."

"Did you not hear me? It's suicide."

"Would you rather we packed up, rowed away and returned home? Call this entire endeavor a failure?"

"It would split the team," Russo muttered.

Alicia eyed them all. She hadn't realized they were so desperate for a win this time. She remembered they'd had a few failures recently, whilst she pursued global enemies with her other team.

"This is your lifelong dream," she said to Crouch. "I get it. But there are times when you just can't win, boss."

"Not this time. Our early successes as the Gold Team may have filled us with a false pride, but we need this. And you, Alicia, I know you're trying to change. To be better. To stop running and face it all head-on. But once upon a time, recently, you'd be calling for an assault on that hill."

She found herself suddenly introspective, weighing his

words. She found that he was probably right. Still, the dangers were no different, still standing and as real as the figures seated around her.

"I'm with you," she said. "I won't walk away. Whatever you guys decide I will do. Fight together, die together, right?"

With difficulty she forced down a yearning to return to her new life, her new man, and a new sense of security.

Crouch stared at the sea, a far-away look on his face. "My own desires shouldn't factor here," he said. "I'd try to pick out a doubloon caught between a kraken's gnashers if it shone bright enough. Russo. Caitlyn. Healey. You decide."

Russo grumbled, not liking being put on the spot. Caitlyn and Healey predictably turned to look at each other.

"We've come a long way," Healey said.

"To get nothing," Caitlyn said.

"And go home empty handed. Again," Healey added.

Alicia snorted. "You two are even finishing each other's sentences now, eh? Shit, there's no hope for you."

"Says the *changed* woman," Russo grumbled.

"Changed, yes," Alicia said. "Turned into a fluffy boxset love-monkey, I will never be."

"Now there's a word I never thought I'd hear you say."

"Fluffy?"

"Love-monkey. It doesn't sound right coming from a bit—"

"Look," Caitlyn interrupted. "We both want to try for the treasure. We came a long way. We beat every clue and found nothing. We have to finish this, right?"

All eyes then turned to Russo, who rather surprisingly nodded immediately in Alicia's direction. "I trust Myles. I'd trust her with my life. She's seen the camp, the men. I go by her instincts."

Alicia blinked in surprise, then felt a little swell of gratitude. No way six months ago would Russo ever have backed her. An incredible accomplishment in itself since a seasoned soldier would take a great deal of convincing.

She watched Crouch's face, feeling sorry for the man's lifelong goal. "It's over, boss. The risk is truly too great."

"Then I guess we head back out to sea," the man said, rising quickly. "No point wasting time here."

Together they rose, largely disappointed but still part of a professional team. Crouch cocked his head as sounds echoed from the camp. First there was shouting and then a volley of gunfire, then more shouting. The men sounded excited, raucous even, as if a new friend had come to play.

Alicia stared hard at Crouch. "Let's see what's going on. Could be a game-changer."

It wasn't. The whole team made their way carefully out of the shelter and through a few stands of trees. Creeping low, they fought off persistent branches, greenery and sneezing fits. They shimmied through dry earth and over ruts and thorn bushes, snagged in inextricable knots. As they reached the edge of the pirates' camp they paused and waited.

Ahead, among the tents, a group of eight men dragged a captive. The man's head was down, his eyes facing the floor and his arms were cut and bruised, bleeding, but it was clearly John Jensen.

"Shit," Crouch hissed. "How the hell. . ? Jensen's SAS."

"No," Alicia cautioned. "Twenty years of crime, debauchery and alcoholism have passed since he belonged to the Regiment. He's just a merc now with a merc's ideals."

"Look," Russo said. "They're questioning him right there."

"You seem surprised," Alicia stated. "These pirates—they have no morals. No grasp of normal life. This is their normal. This is their amusement. They may be stupid, but man, they're bloody dangerous."

Jensen was thrust to his knees and then made to stand. Men

threatened and slapped him. A knife-wielder drew a thin bead of blood from shoulder to shoulder, following the curve of the blade. Another man commented on his tall, rangy stature, likening him to the trunk of a tree. Another pointed out his corded muscle, warning others not to get too close. Weapons were realigned.

A man then appeared, the pirate leader. As filthy and rough-looking as the rest, he wiped sweat from his brow and flicked it at the ground, leaving smear of dirt across his forehead. A broad cleaver hung in one hand, and even from her vantage point Alicia could see it was so encrusted with blood it appeared to be blemished by several layers of dark crimson.

"Who are you?" the pirate leader asked in a voice that explained English was his second language. "You tell or I cut your throat."

The threat wasn't idle. Nobody stood under any illusion. The pirates wanted it to happen. When Jensen didn't answer immediately, the pirate leader stepped forward and pushed his chin up toward the skies.

"I make sure you see your blood soaking your feet before die."

He raised the cleaver as his men took tight hold of Jensen. To a man they were grinning, laughing, jesting at Jensen's expense. To Alicia it was a scene from a circle of Hell, one where demons took immoral men and women to suffer.

She half rose. Crouch pulled her down. Then Jensen shouted out, stilling the blade and the hands and tongues of all those that stood about him.

"A treasure! There's a treasure at the top of the hill. We've . . . I've come for it."

"Y'have?" The leader looked surprised. "What treasure?"

"Pirate," Jensen said, then winced as he remembered where he stood. "Old pirate. Doubloons. Gold. All you could ever want."

"Slice him," one man cried.

"Lying shite just wants to save his own arse." Surprisingly an English accent in the midst of all the others made Alicia wonder just how these assorted, diverse men came to be here right now, in this place, and what made them stick together.

"No. It's right here on this island. Captain Henry Morgan. Heard of him? Sacked a dozen ports or more. This is where he buried it all."

He pointed to the top of the hill. "Up there. Under the tree at the top of the mountain."

The pirates were massed by now, all listening. Russo called out a head count of seventy five. Alicia pointed to the far perimeter of the camp where she saw a new mass of men—most likely Jensen's own well-manned crew.

"Shit," Russo breathed. "This just went crazy."

The battle of Duppy Island and the final race for Captain Morgan's lost, buried treasure began.

## CHAPTER THIRTY SIX

Jensen may well have viewed the world through rum-tinted glasses for the best part of the last decade, but certain skills he'd been taught in his youth never faded away. Getting caught was a momentary lapse. Breaking free was a well-honed skill. The pirate leader doubled over and almost stabbed himself with the bloody cleaver; Jensen kicked him into another man. The nearest found his arm broken, his gun taken and then heard shots being fired. Pirates quickly sobered and jumped away, taking cover as Jensen knew they would.

Not a warrior among them.

He backed away fast, surveying the territory behind and the potential threats. A sniper could never be dismissed but Jensen had no time for that. He sprayed the area in front of him and backed up some more. His men had seen him now, Labadee and Levy sprinting hard and keeping the pirates low with well-placed shots. They were outmanned, but their sudden assault, Jensen's escape and the pirates' general malaise evened the score. The leader was shouting at the top of his voice, thick curses, but at nobody in particular and nobody was listening. The cleaver beat ineffectually at the ground.

Jensen sprayed again and thought he saw a glimpse of figures way across the clearing, bodies moving through the trees. Not pirates. Then . . .

Could be. It could be them.

The race was going to be a tough one. All his life he'd prepared for something like this. Well, not really, but for the last ten years he'd wished to fall lucky just once, take that vast score, and today his numbers were up. Just bad luck it was all going to be in the midst of a firefight.

Labadee and Levy reached his side and he waved them back. "To the woods. Move it!"

Soon they cleared the tree line and melted away without looking back. Jensen raced to the center of his men as he saw Levy hang back to make sure nobody dared follow them. A brief check of the pirate campsite saw them milling back and forth, undisciplined and unsure what to do. Jensen knew it was imperative to take advantage of their confusion.

"Top of the mountain," he said simply. "Any cost. Now."

His men reacted immediately, the mercs a little more slowly. Jensen counted his men as the guys who'd been with him since near the very beginning. Only ten now, several had died recently. But those ten were loyal. The mercs outnumbered them three to one, but the promise of gold made their eyes shine and their brains take a break. Jensen would make sure he put them to the front and the sides of the pack as added insurance for stray bullets. No loss.

He wrapped it up and pointed the way forward. Nobody, not even his lieutenants questioned as to how he'd been captured, let alone what he'd recklessly told the pirates to save his life. Jensen was no coward; he'd faced down unspeakable dangers in his career, but seeing certain, indifferent death in the eyes of a man wielding a blood-caked cleaver? That made a man want to prolong everything, in any way possible. Jensen knew he'd made it all worse.

Still alive though...

And running. He hammered home a magazine into his handgun as he swept past a gaggle of trees, running downhill along a sweeping path and jumping over ruts. To their right the trees frequently thinned and then thickened, offering sporadic views of the pirate camp.

The indolence was lifting. The sullied men were gathering, forming a large hunting party it seemed. Their leader was pointing them toward the great hill with its dangerous obstructions and dense cover. Weapons were being held high and orders were being listened to.

Jensen ran harder, needing to pull out a lead. The man at the top of the hill was going to win this treasure hunt.

King of the mountain?

Shit, the schoolyard game had nothing on this.

"C'mon," he hissed. "Draw your guns and take a bead. Shoot anything that moves that isn't us. We have to reach the top first!"

## CHAPTER THIRTY SEVEN

Alicia saw Crouch struggle with the decision and then make it anyway. His eyes met hers first and asked a question.

"If we do this we do it fast," she said.

He nodded, turned to the front and started sprinting through the trees. Russo loped along in his wake, rifle swinging from a shoulder. Healey and Caitlyn went next and Alicia brought up the rear. Down a slope and then over a small hillock, taking time to skirt the huge, overgrown bole of an ancient tree, scrambling in the undergrowth for a minute and then zigzagging through a thick stand, whipped by branches and almost tripped by concealed roots. Crouch led the team hard, calling on all his training and skills. To their right through the trees the pirate camp was in uproar, more men shouting than listening to their boss, others standing around in bewilderment and not having the awareness to find out. Drugs explained most of the uncertainty, but a lifetime of bullying and persecution also spoke for a portion of it. Alicia guessed that some of these men might not even know who their leader was.

Nevertheless, as Crouch passed the area where the prison tents sat, the pirate camp was starting to mobilize; the men were pointed toward the hill and galvanized to run. Several shots into the air helped. Alicia was forced to concentrate hard on the terrain for a minute as the path twisted and turned and crossed several pitfalls.

Russo, ahead, warned, "Pirates are coming."

Alicia thought of several comebacks but held her breath. The hill might not be a mountain after all, but it was steep and high, and packed with danger. And that was without seventy pirates and forty or so mercs assaulting it. How crazy that their long, hazardous and meandering quest had finished in a race.

How the hell are we ever going to stand our ground at the top if we make it first?

Crouch dropped back through the pack as he fished out his cell and started to make a call. Alicia hoped it would be for reinforcements. Authorities. They couldn't hope to hold out on their own. She stayed behind Caitlyn, keeping an eye on Crouch and now also eyeing Russo in front.

The ground leveled out and then started to rise up, the lower parts of the hill already beginning. Alicia got her first really good daylight look at the slope. It was worse than she had expected. The dangers lay everywhere and promised no easy climb. She called out to those in front.

"Stay together. Watch for dangers. The pirates will hit this hill hard and will pay the price."

"They have the numbers to do that," Russo returned.

"Arrive alive," Alicia intoned. "Always a good motto."

"As good as 'One life, live it'?"

"Nah, that's the best."

"Don't forget Jensen." Crouch panted a little. "He's running up the other side."

"Don't worry." Alicia had no intentions of overlooking the man that had dogged them all the way. "That dude has a long life but a short future."

Healey looked over his shoulder blankly, almost running slap-bang into a tree. "Eh?"

"Means prison," Caitlyn told him. "She means he's going to prison."

"Ahh."

"Zacky boy," Alicia hurdled a double rut that looked like it had been made by a giant tractor wheel, and shook her head.

"One day you'll look back on all this and laugh."

Healey grunted. Alicia loved the interaction between Healey and Russo and herself and even Caitlyn now that she was starting to gel nicely with the main team. Healey was a good soldier and, truth be told, wanted to stay young. It was one of his strengths, a forte she hoped he would never lose. If a grown man could keep a certain innocence, an air of virtue, and never let it go? That was a man she envied.

Upward she ran, the slope steepening with every step. The trees ended and a barren patch of land began that ran around the hill. Suddenly, everyone could see each other and even those oblivious to it all reacted with violence.

The pirates were in the middle and spun both ways. Russo flew to the ground, closely followed by the others. Pirates sprawled headlong as they hit tangled brush, their shots firing dangerously in every direction. To the far right, Jensen's men returned fire, bullets zinging through the pirates and narrowly missing Crouch as he was last to duck.

The cellphone bounced out of his hand.

"Ah, shit. Hope they can track it."

Alicia felt like cursing but used her handgun to bring down two enemies. The smaller pistols were better in this environment. A pirate shot one of his brethren as tripped, then himself through the head as his gun grounded and spun around with his finger still on the trigger. Men around him cringed. Alicia took another down.

Russo crawled hard through the tangled scrub, skirting brambles as best he could and snaking alongside small hillocks. One of the small peaks erupted under the impact of a bullet as he passed, showering him with soil. He kept going.

Healey followed close and then Caitlyn. Alicia made sure she shouted at the researcher to keep her head down, nose to the ground.

An outcropping of rock ahead and Russo was on his knees, drifting around it for shelter. He waited for the others. The pirates ran recklessly ahead, one breaking an ankle in a stony rivulet and left there by his brothers, screaming, unable to get free. Another tried to jump over the outcropping, smashed his head against the bare rock, and fell away unconscious. Alicia saw the leader at the center of the pack still waving his cleaver and offering no direction, no support. She could only make shapes out to the far right. Jensen's men, advancing quickly.

Russo climbed around the outcropping and came to a series of sparse trees. Trunk to trunk he ran, keeping low and covered through open space by Healey. Once Russo had passed the third tree Healey started out, covered by Alicia. In a matter of seconds a fusillade of fire was returned by the advancing pirates, bullets thudding and screaming past. Several punched bark or split air close to Healey, more tore past Alicia, and one slammed off a chunk of boulder close to her left knee. She scrambled back and Healey flattened himself.

Crouch's eyes were on her.

Is it worth it? she wanted to ask. The risk? The loss? The future pain?

But Alicia remained a soldier, and her boss moved ahead. Russo found a space where he could lay down some covering fire and Healey was scrambling off, forcing Alicia to follow. The hot sun blazed down from a cloudless sky and warmed the earth with an unrelenting energy. Dust and pollen wafted around, saturating every deep breath. The sounds of men swearing and crying out in pain, grunting in exertion, and urging their friends on was all she could hear.

The slope steepened. Above, she saw it narrow as it reached up toward the top of the hill. Still, she saw no sign of the tree and suddenly wondered if it even existed at all. What a fine jest for Morgan to pull. What perfect subterfuge. Sending every band of hunters to the top of a laborious slope to find they had done it all for nothing.

But someone knew it was there. The sailors for one. The tree remained to this day a well-known landmark, recognized by locals who plied these waters.

The pirates were spreading out. Mainly due to their numbers and over-enthusiasm, but nevertheless scattering toward the Gold Team. Alicia helped dissuade them with a few well-placed shots. Still, the rival groups pounded hard for the top of the hill, heads down and trading fire.

Jensen's men were closer, possibly encountering some impassable obstacle, and were forced to engage in hand-to-hand combat with half-a-dozen pirates. An Uzi rattled, taking out some of Jensen's men. The leader of the pirates shouted something unintelligible to which nobody reacted.

Alicia paused as a pirate ran hell-for-leather toward Healey. The young lad hadn't even seen the attack. Alicia met the man head on, clubbed him with her pistol, and then kicked him to the ground. He twisted, feeling for a weapon. She shot him and ran on. Crouch raced at her heels.

Up they went. Russo encountered a cave, thought about heading inside and then decided to skirt its black maw. Crouch had a look of indecision in his eyes as he passed but said nothing. Alicia watched it all. Still, she respected and trusted and followed this man. Still, he remained far from perfect.

As was everyone deep inside, but this was a man she had thought different. The toll of his mistakes was heavy and she felt more was to come. But now was definitely not the time.

Ahead, Russo smashed aside a pirate that had forged ahead and doubled back. Healey finished him off, but that didn't bode well for the chase. Alicia saw that the pirates were going to be kings of the mountain, and with their force that would make them pretty much unassailable.

Unless their force somehow went into sharp decline.

She clicked comms and shouted out a plan to Russo.

"Do it," she finished. "Do it now!"

Ramming in a fresh mag she unhooked her rifle and jumped over a ditch and then a fallen log. Russo dropped to one knee up ahead, let off a volley of shots and allowed Healey to pass him by. Then Caitlyn and the rest. Healey now ran at the head of the pack and Russo at the back. Then Healey dropped down, shooting until the others all passed him. Pirates fell and twisted and crashed to the ground, some dead, some with broken bones, all tripping their comrades and getting in each other's way.

Caitlyn dropped alongside Healey and then Alicia was passing them at a leap. She fell to one knee, lined up the pirate pack and then squeezed her trigger. Bullets flew among them, striking flesh and bone, sending gouts of blood high enough to paint a crimson canvas, blocking the sun and falling in errant patterns. Men collapsed face first. Others jumped over their bodies, trying to match Alicia's skills on the run and failing. Always failing. Suddenly she felt Russo galloping by and then the rest of her team and she was up again, forming the rearguard.

The hill below them was littered with the dead, soaked by their life force. Jensen's men added to the dead and took hits of their own. Mercenary met mercenary and forgot their objectives.

Alicia took a moment to look up.

Right to the top of the mountain.

Their goal, the crooked tree and the believed burial site for the most infamous and greatest plundered treasure hoard in history was in sight, and the pirates were in reach of it.

And although they were weary, bruised and bloody, the Gold Team ran harder. And they ran faster. Never had they fought harder for the prize.

## CHAPTER THIRTY EIGHT

The higher slopes were the hardest. The space became narrower and the separate groups grew closer. Mercs came across from Jensen's group, no doubt ordered since Alicia doubted it was the right choice to make, and brought down running pirates in any way possible. Alicia saw some crazy, desperate actions in the next few moments. A pirate turned his gun on a merc only to see the old iron explode in his face as he pulled the trigger. Both men went down. A merc flattened three pirates by barging through their pack with open arms, then slipped off a rocky outcropping and broke his neck on the rocks below. A pirate turned to flee back to camp and was cut down by one of his brethren. Four, then six, then eight pirates reached the top of the hill, started to dance around and fired their guns in the air. Russo took one of them out, and a man that looked distinctly like Jensen killed a second. The pirate leader turned, surveyed the slope and then roared.

Alicia took a potshot, missed, but saw another pirate fall. Good enough. Three pirates now neared them and hopped over a shallow stream to engage. A weapon was leveled. Alicia ducked under and used the barrel to smash the man's nose. A shot was fired. Healey ducked for cover, bobbed up and then shot the man center mass.

Caitlyn tripped and fell before the third.

Looking like all his Christmas presents had come early, he discarded his weapon and pulled out a knife. Alicia shook her head at his stupidity even as she shot him, then helped Caitlyn up.

"Watch your balance."

"I know."

A little sass was good. Alicia engaged a fourth pirate and sent him tumbling back down the hill. Pirates were now climbing to the apex of the hill in numbers—twelve and then twenty and then their leader crested the final rise. Russo was only twenty feet further back but was forced to pull up and take stock.

Pirates ranged around the top of the hill, pointing their weapons down. Their leader barged through them, causing at least two to drop their weapons and have to scramble around on the ground.

"Find me this treasure!" he bellowed.

Alicia picked her way around the obstacles, moving from tree to tree and using boulders to stay safe. The group came together in the lee of a rough rock ledge.

"What next?" Healey said with enthusiasm.

"They have the high ground," Russo said, straight-laced and soldier-like.

"Grenades would be useful," Alicia pointed out.

"Maybe Jensen has some," Crouch said. "Otherwise it's going to be tricky."

Alicia laughed, eyeballing her weapons for damage and changing out the mags. "Conservative as ever, boss."

"King of the Hill was never my forte," he said. "But I say—when Jensen attacks, we attack."

"Would a trained soldier attack that?" Russo motioned toward the rim of the hill guarded by a ring of men.

"It's his ultimate goal in life." Crouch shrugged. "And probably his last chance. He'll attack."

Caitlyn had been resting on her knees. Now she looked up. "How long before the cavalry arrive?"

"To save us?" Crouch pursed his lips. "There are several agencies working in the Caribbean at the moment, some mopping up after the recent Barbados fiasco. The authorities are on their way and, I hope, at least some of those teams."

Alicia took the speech to mean *I don't know.* Sometimes you just had to read between the lines. "Well, they sure as hell won't talk the pirate boss down from there. You can't reason with a man whose major problems have bigger problems of their own."

Crouch eyed her. "True enough. Any ideas?"

"Yeah, let's wait for Jensen to attack first."

A hot sun burned down. Alicia sat with her back to the rocky lee, now able to see the trail of devastation and death that led up the hill. Some men still lived down there, crawling aimlessly. Others were too injured to move. Trees were broken and listing, and scrub was torn apart. Dust still swirled in the air above the paths they had all taken. A fitting aftermath for a crazed, deadly dash into the heart of danger. The Gold Team had engaged with it and executed it well—never in terrible danger and always thinking, always ahead. But the reckless, uncontrolled and ultimately uncaring bunch had made it to the top first and now held all the power. Go figure that life lesson. Her lips curled. Noises filtered through her consciousness. The aggressive protests and instructions from above. The disorganized shooting. The drug-fuelled laughter. Healey and Caitlyn having a whispered conversation. Russo clearing his throat.

She peered up toward the top of the hill, shielded by brush that hung over the ledge. The tree that stood up there by itself was a striking spectacle. Barren, twisted, and gray-white it warped upwards toward the skies, rising magnificent and distorted with misshapen branches and an array of twigs hanging down like broken fingers. It drew her eyes right to the top where the highest boughs appeared to have decided to stop growing, instead curling over and over to form a creepy, lifeless, hanging barrier that reminded her of hundreds of rolls of barbed wire tied together.

"That is one sick tree," she commented.

"Morgan's Fancy," Crouch stated. "That's what it should be called."

"Don't get your hopes up as well," Alicia warned. "This island could be as much a washout as all the rest."

"Has to be here." Crouch thought he'd turned away before she saw the desperation in his eyes. "It *has* to be."

Alicia turned her gaze over to where they thought Jensen had gone to ground. No signs of life existed over there, around the curve of the hill, but then none should. The self-made pirate would be making plans to attack the real modern pirates. She shook her head. Shit, it was becoming confusing.

The Crouch's cell rang. Thinking it was their reinforcements he answered quickly. "Where are you?"

"Just around the corner actually," Jensen's voice came over the lowered loudspeaker.

Crouch started. "How do you have my number?"

"Is that really the issue here? C'mon, Michael. Now, my thinking is that we hit them both at the same time. We were trained by the same people so I know you feel the same."

Alicia fought against accepting the reasonable tones and likening them to Drake. She couldn't think that way now—the men were poles apart.

"You want to join forces?" Crouch was too shocked to think straight.

"No, no, don't be a fool." Jensen laughed. "I want to kill you all for trying so hard to wreck my chances of getting super-rich. But first, neither of us can get to that treasure with the band of idiots in the way. Am I right?"

"I hardly class you as any better."

"Ooh, that hurt. So unnecessary. But I *am* right, Michael. You know it."

Crouch took a look up the hill and then at his team. Alicia knew his decision long before it reached his face. The treasure's influence was all over him.

"I'll meet you at the tree," Jensen said. "I'll kill you there."

Crouch checked his watch. "You ready in five?"

"Let's make it seven. Oh, and as for your number . . . don't forget I have contacts too."

Alicia shook her head at the macho bullshit. She plucked the phone from Crouch's hands. "Just be ready, asshole. We'll go when we're ready."

She threw the object back to Crouch. Then she made sure the rest of the team were watching her.

"Nobody has to do this," she said. "So don't think you do. We can back out right now. After all, it's only buried treasure and the cops are on their way. How far could any of them get?"

"He might rebury it. Sink it. He might have a hidden chopper. A sub—"

"Listen to yourself." Alicia still hadn't forgiven him and embraced the insubordination. "We will decide what is worth risking our lives for. Not you."

Crouch held up both hands.

Russo looked uncomfortable. "We've come this far. Pirates are a ragtag bunch of clowns and jokers. And . . . we finally take down Jensen. I'm in."

Healey looked to Caitlyn and then to Crouch, the two most important people in his life. "I guess Russo's right. Jensen is the big factor here. If we lose him for any reason he could haunt our lives forever. Pop up anytime. I say take him out."

Caitlyn understood the potential for a lifelong threat too. "They're right, Alicia. Never leave an enemy at your back."

She smiled at the words coming from the mouth of the researcher. "I love you all like family," she said. "And respect your decisions, no matter how batshit crazy they are." She gauged the top of the hill. "We ready?"

Russo steadied his rifle. "Ready."

"Spread out," Crouch said. "Don't give them a target."

Alicia felt like reminding him who they were, but bit it back. This wasn't the time. She prepared herself mentally and then moved to the side, following the curve of the ledge around the hill. Then, without a word, she stepped out between it and the next tree and started firing. By the time her bullets reached the top of the hill she was sheltering again behind a thick trunk. Two pirates went down, writhing. Russo followed her lead, taking out two more. Healey went the other way with Caitlyn and felled another. Five seconds later gunfire erupted from the other side of the hill and the pirates started yelling.

Panicked. They didn't even understand they held the better ground.

"Hey!" Guttural shouting rang out. "I foun' dis!"

Alicia moved again, tree to tree, gaining ground. The slope was steep and still hazardous. She stepped over roots and ankle-breaking delves in the earth. A bullet smashed into the tree trunk at her back, the impact passing through her body with a judder. Russo followed, firing constantly. More screams. She peeked around the rough bole and spied the next haven—a body-length delve in the rock. She ran, fired and dived headlong, twisting her body to the shape of the delve and rolling inside. Bullets pounded the area around her. The pirates were slow, but they caught up eventually. Russo took a slightly different route, moving ahead now and making sure she knew it.

"Wanker," she mouthed and rolled to view her next piece of cover. She saw Healey and Caitlyn moving up the hill too, heard Jensen's attack, saw Crouch carefully aiming and picking off the more reckless pirates. Already, they were clearing a gap.

Alicia rose and ran. Two trees this time, and the last before the top of the hill, which now lay about fifteen feet above her.

A pirate charged recklessly, cleaver and rifle held above his head. Alicia could hardly believe his stupidity until spotting the fevered light in his eyes; then took a second to put him out of his misery forever. There was no place in the world for men that shunned compassion, that reoffended their sins without remorse or regret, that cared nothing for humanity.

She spied more cover, probably the last before the summit, but it was good. A cave, a yawning mouth large enough to admit a crouched woman. She had no intentions of exploring, but could use it to make ready for the last assault. Firing now she ran, heard a bullet whizz past her head and another strike a tree three feet to her right. Not great shooting but these guys were more likely to hit her by accident as they aimed for Russo or even Crouch back down the hill. She saw three more fall and roll toward her. Russo knocked down another, now only three steps ahead. The man looked pissed.

Alicia gave him the finger and rolled to her cave; striking a rock with her knee and feeling the fire. She grunted. Dirt rolled off her body. Her tendons ached from the strain and her head hurt with the constant focus required to pull this off. Heat caused sweat to drip into her eyes which she wiped away with earth-caked fingers.

She took a last look at the summit. Glanced over at Russo. "We ready?"

Down the hill Healey and Caitlyn were advancing more slowly, but thinning the herd just as proficiently. Crouch hadn't moved but looked ready, still dispatching the pirates. To their credit the men above had finally realized they were sitting ducks, ranged in a circle as they were, and had found several areas of shelter. But the team—and Jensen's—had taken a fair portion of them down.

Alicia fired above and ran, taking a snaking route and laying down her own cover fire. Crouch helped. And then Russo, doing the same. Bullets shredded the earth at the top of the hill and any foreheads that were crazy enough to pop up. Alicia pressed on, confident she could reach the top before her mag ran dry and already thinking about drawing the handgun. She saw several dangers; pirates to the far left of her trying to crawl into better positions. She diverted her spray momentarily. A head popped up, dispatched by Crouch. She approached the very summit now, ready to engage.

A root caught at her ankles, sending her headlong. She held on to her gun and turned the sprawl into a roll, managing to spin her body right over the curve at the top of the hill, coming around on flat ground and with a full view of the wide, level summit.

She'd left two pirates at her back, but Russo came bounding over the top and soon dispatched them. Alicia took the moment to take it all in. The outlandish tree stood at dead center, a gray, deformed phenomenon. Several figures dug all around it and the pirate leader stood up to his waist in a wide hole, head bent and only his bare back showing. Two pirates sat with their backs to a tree, talking and smoking, guns at their sides, adding to the confusion and sheer peculiarity of the scene. Twelve pirates ranged around the lip of the hill, most now turning their weapons toward her and all at the same time.

Jensen and his three lieutenants burst over the other side of the straggly rim, snagging attention.

Alicia and Russo ran hard for the center of the hilltop, the only logical way to go since it would stop the pirates from shooting as they neared their own men. Healey then crested the brow, Crouch a few steps back. All four of the Gold Team opened fire and felled pirates. The leader popped his head up from the hole and the rest of his body followed.

In his filthy hands he held a strongbox.

Alicia felt her heart drop and her stomach lurch as she leapt into the fray. Jensen ran in from the right with just three men now, the stress showing clear across his face. The assault on the hull had decimated his force, or perhaps some of the mercs had deserted, preferring not to risk suicide.

Whatever it was, Alicia grabbed the shoulders of the pirate in front of her, knowing he would use his machete to attack. She shimmied her body aside, saw the blade pass by, then headbutted the man, spun him to the side and kicked him to the ground. Another came at her, gun up. Alicia ducked low, then came up hard, head under his chin so forcefully she lifted his feet a foot off the ground. He fell hard, unconscious.

Pirates still ran at them from all sides. She dropped her expended rifle and slipped out the all-black Walther. Two men fell, the third barged into her, knocking her off her feet. Alicia rolled and struggled, finding it hard to get a grip of his bare, sweaty skin. Then she saw his hair flapping around in a thick bob and grabbed a handful, jerking it as far back as she was able. He cried out, striking ineffectually with a knife. Alicia shot him and rolled away, rising to her feet.

Only a few strides from the pirate leader now.

Russo came past her. Healey covered Jensen and his three cohorts, who fought the last of the pirates on that side, not as efficiently as the Gold crew it seemed.

The pirate leader held the strongbox above his head. "Wait!"

Clods of earth dropped from his arms and shoulders and the box itself. His face was filthy, his hair hanging rank. Two men lay dead at his side, blood seeping into the grass that surrounded the lifeless tree.

Russo came close to the edge of the recently dug hole. Others lay around with pirates half-crouched inside, hands black with dirt. They had assailed the area fast and hard, mindlessly it seemed. But their frenzied efforts had paid off.

"Wait," Crouch echoed as he came over the brow of the hill,

weapon aimed steadily at the leader's heart. He brought Caitlyn with him, who moved over to Healey's side and pointed her small Glock at Jensen."

"We have to know what's in that box."

"Then wait," the leader of the pirates repeated.

Alicia raised her gun.

## CHAPTER THIRTY NINE

Tension formed a net over the hilltop as concentrated as a localized rain shower. Dozens of pairs of eyes flicked from one face to the next, one trigger-finger to another, evaluating each scenario and every chance. The pressure and friction grew so thick it might form lightning over the warped sentinel that towered above and bore witness to it all, but lightning would never dare strike such a custodian for fear of what it might uncover.

Because the tree still existed at all, it had to exist for a reason.

Ghost Island, Alicia thought as she assessed every angle. Well, now you have a far larger membership.

She saw the remaining half-dozen pirates lower their guns. Saw the leader unarmed and unprotected in the hole. Watched as one of Jensen's lieutenants—Forrester she thought—drew down on Healey and fell with a hole through his chest. That left Jensen, now angrier than ever, and two men. She saw Crouch advancing from the corner of her eye, heading straight for the strongbox. She saw Jensen strain his every sinew to get a better view. Silence descended again for a long minute.

Violence gripped hard to the edge of the curtain of tension. Soon, Alicia knew, it would break through.

"You take it," the pirate leader snarled at Crouch. "Here, for you."

He placed it on the edge of the hole, at Crouch's feet. The boss evaluated the leader, saw no immediate threat, and moved back, dragging the dirty box with him. From her own vantage point, Alicia could see its appearance was terribly familiar—

the same as all the others they had found. The next few minutes didn't bode well.

All this death. This struggle. This expectation.

All for naught.

Crouch moved to the side of the box, blocking Jensen's view, and fell to his knees. A deep breath came next and a quick glance at Alicia. Then, he broke the lock and lifted the heavy lid.

Absolute silence. Bated breath. Every man and woman waited to see what Crouch would find.

Alicia saw no sign on his face. Then he placed his hands inside the box, scooped something up and lifted it high for all to see.

"The treasure of Captain Henry Morgan," he said.

Alicia stared hard, biting her bottom lip. It was a tangled bunch of trinkets, as she'd expected and just like all the ones that came before. It was a guilty hoard, a local offering. It was disappointment to the treasure hunters that came next.

"No gold." Jensen's legs wobbled. "There is no gold?"

The pirate leader sat down despondently in the hole. Only his head could be seen. His men drooped. Alicia saw Caitlyn walk across the clearing, heading for Crouch's side. Nobody else moved and the only sound was the slither of gold chains through Crouch's shaking fingers.

"Is there nothing else?" the researcher asked. "It strikes me as odd that this final clue, not recorded on Morgan's maps, lead us to another strongbox. He wanted only the committed and the worthy to find this."

Crouch let the jewelry fall back inside the box and rooted around in the depths. "We failed." He was muttering obliviously. "Failed again."

Caitlyn fell beside him and put a hand over his. "Stop. Let me look."

She bent over the box. Alicia continued her surveillance of the hilltop, wishing now they'd dispatched more men. The numbers up here were still a little daunting.

Caitlyn pulled a sheet of parchment from the strongbox. "What's this?" She laid it on the grass and unfolded it.

Crouch peered over her shoulder. "A letter. Is it written by Morgan?"

Caitlyn glanced around at all the watchers, saw no way of imparting the information that wouldn't result in bloodshed, so lowered her head and began to read aloud.

"I, Henry Morgan, here leave behind the last of the treasures that blacken my conscience. There is no more, and nothing left for me. I set sail now on my final voyage and with everything that I own, to the place of my birth and to England, there to meet a date with the gallows. I have regrets, but regrets always outlive the men that harbor them."

"Just a final note?" Russo said. "Now there's a letdown."

"A goodbye," Alicia said. "Seems odd."

"Remember that Morgan was recalled by the English after sacking Panama," Caitlyn reminded them. "He broke the peace treaty between England and Spain and was recalled to face a trial. His pirating days came to an end right then."

"Privateer." Jensen took a step forward so that he was now in the open. "The English made the treaty with Spain without Morgan's knowledge. So, in effect, he was a privateer until then, and only became a pirate when he attacked Panama—even though he didn't know it at the time."

"It hardly matters," Crouch rooted again in the box as if expecting another map to pop out of a secret compartment. Caitlyn again gently laid her hand atop him.

"There is nothing more, Michael."

"A name is but a title," Alicia said then. "It doesn't change the person beneath. A politician can be a crook. A finance manager a thief. A hedge fund manager a con man. Huh." She grimaced. "And Wall Street bankers can be all of those things, I guess."

Caitlyn rose and pulled Crouch up with her, leaving the box. She reread the letter and googled Morgan's signature to make sure it matched. The hilltop still bristled with an unrelenting apprehension. Alicia started to wonder how their own team and then two highly strung, murderous crews might hope to withdraw peaceably from the situation.

Maybe they could back away and let the other two have at it.

She glanced at Russo who appeared to be thinking along similar lines. He nodded toward the edge. Healey nodded too. Then she saw Jensen looking at them.

We have to take him with us.

Jail time was maybe too good for him, but she couldn't just kill a man, even one such as he. It felt good now to know that once she'd had no such compunctions. Every day, she moved further ahead.

Caitlyn came over with a dejected Crouch carrying the strongbox. Nothing else moved. Caitlyn looked at both Alicia and Russo.

"So whilst searching for Morgan's sig I came across the tales that followed his recall to England and followed his journey. Not one of them mentions him returning to his homeland."

Alicia frowned. "You're speaking riddles. England is his homeland. That's why he returned at her request to face trial."

"No." Caitlyn smiled. "England was not Morgan's homeland. He was born in Wales where his family had a large farm. Now, none of the accounts mention that he returned to Wales. Take that in context with what we just read and you have . . . ?"

"Can barely remember," Russo said. "Busy here."

"All right. The relevant part goes 'I set sail now on my final voyage and with everything that I own, to the place of my birth and to England, there to meet a date with the gallows.'"

Out of context and with the new information, Alicia understood without any further prompting. She stared at

Crouch and the abrupt hope in his eyes. "You believe that Morgan finally finished his guilt-trip here and then set sail supposedly for England with his entire treasure hoard?"

"The sentence alludes to it," Caitlyn said. "And Morgan would do it. From everything we know of him, you know he would. He told them he sailed straight for England, but stopped off in Wales and returned home. Either by force, or bribery or sheer charisma, Morgan is one of history's most charismatic men, able to lead so many in such harsh circumstances, for so long, and with such success. The facts are all here."

Alicia had no illusions that Jensen was listening to their reasoning, but now wasn't the time to deal with the crook. "And the family farm? Don't tell me it's still there today?"

"I still think it's a stretch," Russo grumbled. "And Wales is a long way and can freeze the balls of a brass monkey."

Alicia grunted. "Is that a pirate expression?"

"Yeah, but who gives a fuck?"

"Of course I haven't mentioned the real reason we should believe the treasure went all the way to Wales," Caitlyn said sweetly, then paused.

Even Alicia leaned forward, along with every pirate and self-proclaimed leader.

"Simple—Henry Morgan thought he was going to die. He believed he would be put to death for his crimes against the Crown in London."

"And clearly he still hoarded his treasure, right up until then." Crouch suddenly had a thrill in his voice. "Right until this letter was written. So, not wanting the Crown to seize and squander his treasure, he took it home, and buried it there."

Caitlyn bowed. "You read my mind."

And then the hilltop finally erupted in violence.

Jensen had heard enough and dived for a nearby boulder, screaming at his two remaining lieutenants to open fire. The pirate leader rose up out of the hole, shedding earth and mud, a fearsome sight with an Uzi suddenly grasped in each hand. Alicia saw it and knew Crouch had missed it; one more mistake. Before anyone could react, bullets were lacing the air.

Caitlyn fell to the ground under fire, screaming.

Healey dived in front of her, a tad late but staying put.

Alicia dropped and drew her Walther. Incredibly though, the pirate leader's head exploded as Labadee and Levy fired at him. The body slumped just as the remaining pirates found their wits and their guns.

Alicia flicked a glance at Caitlyn. "You okay?"

"I'm good. Not hit."

Healey rolled off her. Russo fired at the pirates that were charging as if playing a game. All fell, tumbling and bloodied to the grass. One spun under fire and smashed head-first into the resolute tree, leaving a smear of blood on the bark. Jensen scrambled for the edge of the hilltop as Labadee and Levy turned their weapons on the Gold Team.

Too late. Alicia and Russo were already within striking distance. Alicia took the big Jamaican, wrestling with his gun. The man was strong and tussled hard, muscles bulging. Alicia used his own force against him, turning the limbs so that they would break. Labadee barely managed to stop in time, but then became redundant, doing nothing. Alicia pushed him away for space, then delivered a double blow to the face and to the chest. She kicked his knee so that he fell hard on his good one. She jumped in with a right knee that connected solidly with his nose.

And was left standing, her opponent battered and out cold at her feet.

Russo tangled with Levy, dodging knife blows, catching two on his own Walther which he used as a metal shield. The knife thrusts came fast and deadly, but Russo turned them all. Alicia came up close.

"Need help, fat boy?"

Russo glared, then saw Levy's knife nick a sliver of flesh from his right arm. When the next attack came he fell to his knees, brought the gun around and simply shot Levy in the gut. Fight over. Alicia let out a breath.

"Was wondering why you just didn't shoot the cock-end."

"I needed the practice," Russo whined. "Haven't been in a knife fight for months. And who the hell are you calling fat boy, you dumb bitch?"

"Ooh, Robster. You really need to work on those insults. And loosen up. I'm just pulling your leg. If you haven't figured that out by now, boy, you surely never will."

"I've known a few bit—"

But Alicia was no longer listening.

Her eyes had fixed on Caitlyn Nash and her distraught face. And then on Crouch's which was fixed in an expression of utter agony.

And then she knew.

## CHAPTER FORTY

For Alicia there was no hilltop, no weather, no hot sun and no grass. There was no lofty, malformed tree. There were no surroundings, no thought, not even a single ounce of breath. Everything in her world encompassed a single solitary figure.

Zack Healey.

The youngest of them all, the one with the most promise. Healey loved Caitlyn. And Healey had thrown himself in front of her when the pirate leader opened fire. They all assumed because Caitlyn was fine the pirate had shot wide, and then they went instantly into action. They never thought Healey had taken the bullets.

Alicia fell at his side now, tears streaming down her face. Caitlyn leaned over the dead man's body, heaving, her breaths as ragged as a serrated blade. Crouch stared at Healey's ashen face in horror, every feature frozen.

Alicia reached out a hand, watched as her fingers trembled. "Zack?"

Russo, the big, gruff hard man, fell alongside his friend and sobbed, moans wracking his entire body. He placed a huge arm across Healey's shoulders and buried his face into the ground. Caitlyn crawled closer and held on so tight she might never move again.

The sun waned in the western skies. No sound existed save for the team's misery and the seeping of blood into the hard ground. Not from one but from over a hundred men.

In the end it was the helicopters that moved them. They might have stayed there the rest of the day and all night, into the next dawn, but the blood-red sunset heralded the choppers filled with police and agencies that Crouch knew, and made them sit back, stare up into the skies—see the clouds and the glorious sunset and the yellow sunshine that their colleague would never see again—and consider all they had lost.

It was true that you didn't value what you had until you realized that someone close to you would never see it again. From the most wondrous trip to the swings in your garden. From the greatest, free feeling to the picture of your children on your mantelpiece. One day, there every day, taken for granted—the next something you just can't grasp anymore and wished you'd given more of yourself to.

I will see it all for you. Alicia rose from Healey's body, face red and streaked. And I will never say no to or push aside the people I love ever again.

Crouch looked up into the crimson sunset. "I . . . I don't know what to do next."

Caitlyn rose with him, slowly, shakily, her own face turned upward. "We finish what we all started. We finish this as a team."

Alicia turned away, eyes brimming anew.

## CHAPTER FORTY ONE

The flight to Wales was long and subdued, the team at first all lying back, trying to come to terms with Healey's death and their own feelings, not to mention their own weariness after such a long, intense battle. Those that could, ate. Those that wanted to, consumed alcohol. Others downed sugary drinks because they knew sleep was days away. At first the jet slipped through the clouds in silence, each member of the Gold Team lost in their own reveries, but then Caitlyn crept next to Crouch and Russo came over to Alicia. Soon, they were whispering and then meeting each other's eyes. Then they were feeling a little comforted as they saw the shared grief in faces like mirror images.

As the journey stretched from painful to insufferable, Caitlyn eased its passing by reading out everything she could find about Henry Morgan's hometown. "Since he was known as the greatest of all the 'brethren of the coast', Wales and its storytellers appear to have embraced Morgan's tale. He was born at Llanrumney Hall on his father's farm in 1635. It's in Monmouthshire. And of course he died, *Sir* Henry Morgan, having been knighted for his . . . actions all along the Spanish Main. Interestingly, Monmouthshire borders both part of the South Wales coast and England, making it easy to slip into and out of."

"And Llanrumney Hall?" Crouch asked. "His home. Does it still stand?"

Caitlyn hesitated, a far-away look hitting her eyes and a tear starting to form. Crouch reached out to touch her hand. "I'm so sorry."

Alicia felt Russo wilt a little beside her, reached out and put an arm around the big man's shoulders. She had never offered so much of herself emotionally to anyone except one man. Russo smiled as best he could.

"It may still stand," Caitlyn finished after an unknown time. "Llanrumney Hall was turned into a pub long ago. It's still there."

"So we end all of this in a pub?" Alicia said. "That'll do. I hope to God it has lodgings too, 'cause I'll be drinking the place dry."

"Won't help," Crouch said.

"For an hour or two it will," Alicia said. "And I'll deal with the rest head on."

"We all will. Together," Russo said.

"Wonder if it sells rum?" Alicia said, then added, "I thought Healey might have said that."

It brought the slightest relief to all their faces. "That he would," Crouch said and Caitlyn nodded.

The plane flew fast through the night, chartered by the team's benefactor and totally private. It was a fast jet, since they had lost many hours with Healey and then the cops, giving Jensen the chance to find a way to Britain if he chose to do so. Indeed, a later check of one of his aliases showed he had done just that.

And the location of Morgan's home wasn't exactly private knowledge.

Alicia counted the hours down, flicked her mind through what she knew of Healey's past and tried to be a comfort to Russo and the others. Very soon she would have to return to her primary unit. The toll of this mission was going to make everything harder—every problem she would have to deal with back there and every outcome.

"This is the last location for me," Alicia told them whilst she had the chance. "If all this leads to is another note, or letter, I can't promise I'll tag along."

Crouch looked hurt. "Not running away?" he asked, an unnecessarily hurtful charge.

"No," she said simply, easily. "Going home. If you can, maybe you guys should too. At least for a short while."

She thought about their pasts and then grimaced. Caitlyn had no remaining family and neither did Crouch. She didn't know about Russo, but Alicia considered her team her family so maybe they should actually stick together.

"Actually, scratch that last comment," she said. "Who the hell am I to be handing out advice? Not a rebel without a cause—more a lost girl without a clue."

Russo finally managed a smile. "Never a truer word came out of your mouth."

"Thanks, Rob. I really needed that."

"Huh? No jaunty nickname?"

"I'm all out of nicknames, Rob. I'm just with my friends right now."

## CHAPTER FORTY TWO

Wales lies at the western side of the United Kingdom, a rugged country composed largely of mountains and coastline. They ordered the jet to land at Cardiff Airport and then rented a car to travel the last leg of their journey to Llanrumney Hall. The roads were blacked out as it passed the witching hour, snaking, hedge-lined byways lit only by the stark crescent moon. The team sat together in the Range Rover, an acute feeling for the one person missing cutting each one of them as deep as a razor.

Alicia stared out the window at a darkness that threatened to engulf them all, the only relief the odd pool of light offered by a random streetlamp or the distant lights shed by a solitary house or farm. Crouch drove by the directions offered by the satnav, following one twisting route after the other and passing only a single car coming in the opposite direction. They could have been the only people left alive in the world, traveling the lonely, unsociable darkness forever and a day.

Alicia fought off a feeling that this was all wrong. Bouncing from Jamaica and Haiti and Panama to a small Welsh tavern didn't fit—it didn't fit with Henry Morgan and it didn't fit with the tales of his storied treasure hoard. But then, maybe that's why it was never found.

A night in Wales on his way to England. Who would know? Only those that helped, and they would only be well-trusted and well-paid men, able to strike off alone to live out their days in luxury. Either that or Morgan murdered them all in Llanrumney Hall. Either story could be true.

The car crunched slowly up a gravel drive and approached a

wall of trees. Darkness was now a palpable thing, pressing down amidst all the wilds of the Welsh countryside. And then came a totally unexpected thing.

Llanrumney Hall, an enormous pub out in the middle of nowhere, known and visited by all but still a kept secret. Alicia wondered if there were many that knew this once belonged to the Morgan estate as she marveled at the size of it. White-walled, three-storied and with a flat roof, it had been built in the fifteenth century. All the more surprising because it fitted in at the end of an unremarkable tree-lined lane, the pub stood dimly lit now, its windows dark save for the odd lit lamp, its doors closed and barred against the ungodly hour.

After all, brigands rode the night didn't they? Especially in Wales, the home of the greatest of them all.

Alicia studied the great pub and its surrounds. A smaller structure lay to the left and other houses beyond a fence. To the right an open field, also bordered by a fence. Crouch crunched into the car park and found a space, left the engine running.

"Ideas?"

Caitlyn never stopped thinking. "They turned this place into a pub in 1951. Before that it was a residence, presumably much unchanged from the original structure. It's a Grade I listed building."

"Some things will have changed," Crouch insisted.

"Agreed. But where, logically, would a pirate *not* leave his treasure?"

Crouch studied the pub. "Bedrooms," he said. "Loft. Anything above the ground floor. He would want it safe, dry, and unlikely to be found accidentally. That leaves the grounds—" he studied what he could see "—which are nothing more than flat earth. Possibly a hidden trapdoor?" He shrugged. "Or the house itself. Shall we see?"

Alicia hesitated. "It's three in the morning."

"Perfect," Crouch said. "We have reason to do this. We're in the UK, my stomping ground. We're checking no unsavory sorts have come before us." He looked over at Alicia. "Want me to continue?"

"Not even a little bit." She reached for the door handle. "Let's do this."

The team exited the Range Rover and assumed a formation. Hands hovered near weapons they had brought with them from Jamaica. Crouch's contacts and Alicia's Special Agency ID had their uses, after all. Dark patches away from the house moved slowly, causing Russo to hiss for silence. Slowly, he crouched, staring at the dark.

"Careful." He put a hand up as Alicia walked by.

"It's just sheep," she told him. "Wales is full of 'em. Is it the big furry ones that scare you, or the bare, shaven skinny ones?"

"Shit." Russo rose and faced the house without a hint of acknowledgement. Crouch headed for the rear and the back door, moving carefully and hugging the side of the building. Alicia followed, eyes flitting and trying to penetrate the black shroud. Noises came from the far field, animals moving, and the call of night creatures. Around the back of the pub they found an extensive patio area with benches, seating and a huge barbecue. Outdoor heaters stood around every table, chained to the floor.

Crouch hugged the wall. Alicia looked up and to the side, leaving nothing to chance. They moved soundlessly, and the chill Welsh night pressed around them. Alicia saw breath stealing from Crouch's mouth as he walked, a wild contrast to where they had come from. Her fingers were cold on the trigger.

Crouch stopped. Alicia glanced around his body.

"That's not a good sign."

The pub's rear door had been forced, the frame broken. Light flooded out from the room beyond but no alarm had been tripped. Alicia could only assume Jensen had managed to find a local thief to do the job, unless he'd somehow learned burglary skills during his many travels. Possible.

"It could be unrelated," Caitlyn said.

Alicia didn't believe in such coincidence, but kept her silence. She pushed ahead of Crouch and beckoned Russo over. "Be ready."

Inch by inch, she used her left hand to push the door open, revealing an interior hallway. Narrow and lit at the far end it was cluttered with a vast array of items in boxes and plastic containers. The door at the far end was closed.

She inched along, allowing the team to form behind her. The far door opened with a faint click and then they were inside a softly illuminated kitchen area. Alicia went first and then the others spread out. Pots and pans hung at head height and a large industrial fridge-freezer filled one corner. A central worktop bench almost cut the room in half and a double sink sat near the exit door. The whole area was quiet, the lights dim but still enough to ensure they were totally alone. Russo crouched down to the floor and hissed for attention.

Without a sound he pointed at three sets of dusty footprints overlaying the pristine floor. A set of trainers, a pair of boots and a smaller set of trainers. Alicia felt a rush of fear not for herself but for the men, women and children lodging here. No telling what Jensen might do. Carefully, she placed a hand on Crouch's shoulder.

"Shouldn't we get everyone out?"

"Probably." The boss sent a longing glance after Russo. "But I'd like to know where we're going first before we warn Jensen."

Alicia considered it. The truth was, the footsteps might not be

Jensen at all. Another truth was, this could be yet another wild goose chase.

It felt right though. Validation ran right through the bricks and mortar of this place, from its fifteenth-century foundations to its connection to Morgan and the subterfuge surrounding his last voyage. A man knowing he was going to his death wouldn't take his spoils all the way to the government's front door now would he?

She nodded. "Ten minutes."

They crept through the kitchen and entered a large, mahogany paneled room with a pool table at the center. Chairs lined the walls and a darts- and chalkboard too. Some kind of function room. Russo pointed to the bare floor and retreated, soon silently padding into another room with high, curtained windows, tables and several armchairs scattered about. Darkness was their nemesis here, drowning out their small flashlights as they looked around. Again, nothing appeared out of place and no footprints lined the floor. Russo led the way through two more rooms as the minutes ticked away.

"Boss, we gotta do this right," Alicia said finally. "Lights on. People out. We're blind here."

They switched around and headed back to the kitchen. Crouch turned on the lights as the others leaned against worktops. Alicia got a better look at the dusty prints and noted that they never actually left the room.

Crouch clucked and smiled. "Look at this, guys."

Alicia was talking to Caitlyn. "Any chance you can use that magic of yours to find an old blueprint of this place? We need to separate the old from the new."

"Not a chance, I'm afraid. Info regarding Llanrumney Hall is pretty sparse around the Net and Google Maps can't penetrate through walls." She shrugged and added: "Yet."

"That we know of," Crouch pointed out and then caught their attention. "How about this?"

Alicia looked across to see a small, red fire alarm button. Russo frowned. "You think it'll open a secret door?"

"No. But I do think it will clear the place out."

"Ah, yeah. Good idea."

Crouch pressed the button and listened to the klaxon sound of alarm bells. Lights started to go on and, after a few minutes, the sound of feet descending the stairs and sleepy voices could be heard. Someone was trying to calm the residents down and a man's voice stated that he was "off back to bed". The team saw more and more illumination as they watched through the open kitchen door.

Crouch was wasting no time though. As soon as he had pressed the alarm he enlisted Russo's help and started moving units. Alicia took a different stance on the matter, checking the floor for scuff marks. Caitlyn examined the walls and inside cupboards. It stood to reason that the kitchen would be the oldest room in the house, but after five minutes they had found nothing. Alicia took another careful look at the footprints as they watched people start to walk toward the front doors.

"They do actually leave the kitchen area," she said. "Look."

Outside, the residents and landlord of the pub noticed people standing in the kitchen. Some started drifting over. The bulk of them milled around as many started to question the fire's authenticity. Alicia shook her head. "If it were a real fire some of these people would wait to go crispy duck before they started to run."

They followed the prints again, ending at a dark-wood paneled wall in which was set a six-foot high door. Crouch reached out to push it open.

As it moved inward a red wire stretched, a fuse exploded and an incendiary device went off. The door had been booby trapped from the inside. The entire house plunged into darkness.

"Damn, he's prepared for us."

Screams sounded out from behind. Men yelled for someone to get the doors open. In utter darkness, the house and the countryside took on a more menacing aspect. As Alicia watched a man fell over, struck his head on a table and didn't get up. A woman screamed. "He's dead! He's dead! He just fell. Oh God, there's a killer among us!"

So much for the power of television. Without hesitation someone lifted a vase and threw it through a patio door window. Someone else wrenched at the frame, drawing blood and shrieking. A young man saw the blood and leaped away.

Crouch pushed open the door and looked down, shone his flashlight. "Appears to be a cellar. Some steep steps here so watch out."

The team descended into the inky, creepy blackness, taking care and wondering what might lurk in the far corners of the room. Pitch black and utter silence fell over them, making Alicia feel smothered. The stairs were their only safe harbor, the rest of the room could have been a pit leading straight to Hell. Russo took point, followed by Crouch, Caitlyn and Alicia, who made sure she closed the door at their backs. They didn't want anyone falling through an open door by accident.

"Watch out for any other traps," Crouch said.

Russo grunted, finally reaching solid ground. The cellar was a vast place, the walls just rock and chipped stone, with the roots of a desiccated tree running through. Alicia immediately got an impression of age, refuted by the modern strip-lights and piles of boxes, cans and drinks, but it was the overlying feel of the place that spoke to her bones. This cellar had been hewn at the same time they built the house.

Still, it was just one big oblong room. No passageways leading further underground. No doors that they could see. And no clear footprints to follow.

"Split up," Crouch said. "Examine every nook and cranny."

Alicia brushed a spiderweb away to reach into a far corner. The walls were solid. Caitlyn called them over to investigate a niche at the bottom of the far wall, but no seams were evident. They moved boxes and crates but found nothing, the light from their tiny flashlights barely any use at all. In the end, Crouch sat on a crate and let out a long, frustrated breath.

"What are we missing?"

"Dinner," Alicia breathed back. "I really missed that last night, and pretty soon I'm gonna be missing breakfast too."

"Proper tools would help," Caitlyn said. "We could check for spaces behind these walls."

"An awful lot can happen in four hundred years," Crouch said. "Maybe *this* was where Morgan left his treasure."

"And somebody found it? Kept it quiet?"

Crouch shrugged. "Maybe. It would be a fitting end to this bloody quest."

"I don't think so," a voice said from the shadows. "It would be too damn easy, Michael."

Jensen leapt for Crouch, aiming for the man's throat. The deeper shadows erupted with figures, arms and legs and twisted faces, like demons leaping up from the caverns of Hell. They wielded knives and their eyes flashed in the reflected flashlight beams. Alicia stumbled back in shock, tripping over Caitlyn and falling to the floor. Russo almost managed to cover a little shriek, at the same time stumbling across a crate of water bottles.

The fiends were upon them.

## CHAPTER FORTY THREE

Crouch struggled to breathe, gasping. Jensen squeezed harder, intent on watching his opponent's face turn from pink to red, purple to black. His own face was feral, possessed. Alicia kicked out as shadows flitted to and fro through the meagre pinpricks of light. One struck at her leg and then her ribs, making her groan. One more kicked Caitlyn in the mouth, drawing blood. Caitlyn fell back, striking her head on the floor.

Alicia groaned, saw another motion of dark and managed to block a harsh blow. The flashlights were rolling around and useless, the demonic figures somehow used to the dark. It was chaos, savage, malevolent. It was the nameless and the unfamiliar that disrupted their focus. Alicia had never been in such a situation, faced with enemies that she could not identify nor clearly see. The bizarreness of it all beat at her as hard as any fist.

Crouch fell off the crate he'd been sitting on, causing Jensen to lose his grip and utter a curse. That single act penetrated Alicia's odd fugue.

Darkness struck at her.

Alicia caught its left boot, twisted, and threw it sprawling to the floor. Listened to it cry out in pain. Saw it rise up in the shape of a young man and hit it hard around the ribs. A crack attested to its fallibility, a scream to its humanity. She smashed its throat with her elbow, wrestled the knife away and then searched the face for clues.

Night goggles.

She wrenched them away, threw them immediately to Caitlyn. "Call it!"

A patch of night struck her chest, then her face. Alicia tasted blood. No need to call this one. Three strikes and the apparition was down, passing again through rolling flashlight beams, shapeless and alien. Caitlyn pushed the goggles over her head and began to shout instructions.

"Russo! Two feet dead right. Coming at you. Alicia, at your feet, rising now. Michael, take that fucker down!"

Crouch rolled and rolled, finally breaking Jensen's hold. Though bruised and panting he wasted no time in recovery, just kicked out and rolled again. Still keeping hold of his flashlight, he shone the light straight into Jensen's eyes.

The head whipped away, the goggles flaring. Crouch launched an attack faster than an RPG, crashing into Jensen's midriff and taking him to the ground. Caitlyn whipped her head back to where Alicia and Russo struggled.

"Behind you, Alicia. Three, two, one... Russo—duck!"

With the ongoing instruction and the sure knowledge of what they fought, the soldiers soon showed their superiority. Alicia realized they faced local thugs high on something. But their blood flowed as well as any enemy's. Russo finished his last opponent, winded and slashed, but went immediately over to where Crouch fought Jensen.

Alicia, maddened by the shadowy battle and uncertain source of it, annoyed with herself for succumbing to doubt, picked her final opponent up by the hair and launched him bodily at Russo.

"Here. Throw that in the bloody bin."

Russo caught the human projectile, hefted and increased the momentum, flinging him across the room and into a ceiling-high, double-row of old barrels. Alicia watched them fly apart, timbers sparring away, as she jumped to Crouch's aid.

Dark liquid flooded the cellar floor as the local thug groaned. Crouch found a blow that struck under Jensen's chin, snapping his head back and sending him to the floor. Caitlyn gathered up all the flashlights and made a double-sweep of the cellar.

"No more... Welsh fairies."

Crouch pushed his body to its knees and crawled over to Jensen's side, voice rasping. "Where?" he grated. "Where's the goddamn treasure?"

"Dunno," Jensen all but laughed. "We were waiting for you."

Crouch's head hit the floor. "Bollocks."

Caitlyn passed night goggles out among the team. Everyone slipped a pair on and then sat back on their haunches. Truth be told, to Alicia, everything looked pretty much as she'd expected. No secret doors or hidden ledges, no suspicious veins in the rock. The floor looked solid, but she guessed they'd have to move everything aside to get a proper take.

Caitlyn's voice was a whisper. "Guys."

Crouch looked up, face creased, old and bloodied, eyes only for Jensen. "At least you will get all you deserve," he said. "And a long time coming."

"I escaped once..." Jensen rasped.

"Guys..." Caitlyn said a little louder.

Alicia reached out for Russo. "You okay there, Rob? Look a bit cut up."

The big soldier held his arms out, streaked with blood. "One of those sneaky bastards got past me. Early on." He added the last as if that explained the slip-up.

"Um, guys..."

The door at the top of the stairs opened. A man looked down, saw the figures and perhaps the blood in the flashlight beams. His next words: "I'm calling the police!" confirmed it.

"Thanks," Crouch said and meant it.

*"Fuck! Guys!"* Caitlyn screamed so loudly now Alicia jumped a foot off the floor.

"What the hell is it?"

The researcher just pointed. Alicia followed her gesture and saw the unfortunate man Russo and she had thrown against the wall. And the stack of barrels. It was the barrels that drew the interest though. Destroyed, splintered and leaking a dark liquid Alicia could only guess to be rum, they revealed that which had been hiding behind their heavy bulk.

A door. Clear through the goggles, but invisible in half-light. Crouch stared hard at it.

"Could be," he muttered excitedly. "Could be."

Alicia felt hope but then Russo dashed it. "I find it hard to believe it's been there four hundred years behind all those barrels."

"So do I," Crouch said with half a smile. "So ask yourself why all those hefty barrels are stood in front of it."

Russo's lips moved but nothing came out. Alicia pondered the rather interesting line of reasoning.

"Because when it became a pub the new owner checked behind it . . . and found nothing?"

Crouch nodded. "Let's go see."

They slogged through the spilt rum, finding it a little ironic considering in whose footsteps they were following, and wrenched open the locked door after finding a crowbar. They took Jensen with them, held by Russo. Crouch flung the door open and used the night-vision goggles to peer inside.

"Well, it's a storage room, I guess. But small. So small you'd be hard-pressed to fit more than a few crates in here."

Crouch sounded depressed. Alicia handed him the crowbar. "Dig around for a bit."

Under the six-hundred-year-old pub, under the very earth that had once belonged to Captain Henry Morgan's father; inside the dwelling where the young boy had grown and returned only once as a man and a condemned pirate, the Gold

Team dug and pounded and searched. They gouged every wall, slammed every surface. They broke bricks apart, shattered stone. Crouch wedged the wrecking bar further and further into a hole he'd made and eventually found no more resistance.

"People," he said. "I just found air."

Air was good. It meant there was space beyond the broad wall that made up the back of the storage room.

"Six blocks thick." He panted. "If I hadn't been so bloody desperate I would never have kept going."

The dark, old, untouched mortar came apart. The stones fell inward. Crouch passed them to the others, working hard and sweating profusely. Soon a space had been made large enough to fit his head and shoulders through. The boss then turned to Caitlyn.

"Would you like to do the honors? For Zack?"

She smiled and nodded, fitted her slender top-half into the hole and looked around. When she returned she took off the goggles and flashed a pair of eyes so bright they might light up the cellar.

"A tunnel," she said as if it were a golden headdress. "Wide enough for all of us and descending slightly. Shall we?"

They dragged Jensen between them, forcing him into the gap though, in truth, the man appeared eager to tag along. Probably still looking for a chance to get free, Alicia knew. But then maybe he also wanted to see Henry Morgan's treasure.

Far from the place he called home. Far from the place Morgan called home. How ironic. Alicia wondered how many times Morgan had pined for it, yearned for it as he sailed back and spent those years governing Jamaica. Maybe the man actually died of a broken heart.

The tunnel was hard on the palms and knees but spacious enough. It angled downward and grew warmer at first, then decidedly cold. Crouch thanked Jensen for the night-vision goggles. They certainly wouldn't have been able to progress so quickly without them.

At length, they came to what could only be described as a chute. A wide passage down that was vertical enough to ask a whole lot of faith for any would-be explorer.

"Whoa," Alicia eyed it doubtfully. "We should chuck the criminal in first."

Jensen wriggled.

Crouch held a hand up. "As you said previously, Alicia, we're in this because of me. Because of my lifelong search for long lost treasure. I'll take the plunge."

Nobody offered up any objections. Crouch maneuvered himself so that his legs dangled over the edge and then looked back. "Cross everything."

"Good luck," Alicia said and meant it.

The boss pushed himself away, falling down the chute and unable to stop a shriek escaping from his throat. Alicia glanced at Russo.

"You think that was a happy shriek? Or a *fuck me, I'm dead,* shriek?"

Russo shrugged. "Hard to tell apart. You've heard both, I take it?"

"Well yeah, but only in the bedroom."

Russo turned away. The team heard a scraping from below and then Crouch's thin voice echoing back up.

"It's . . . okay. Come on down."

Alicia jumped up first. "He doesn't sound so sure, so let's get this over with."

She pushed herself off, gliding fast down the rocky tunnel, gathering speed and feeling her body start to shift from side to side. She tried to arrest the momentum. The chute was incredibly smooth. Gray rock flashed past her goggles, unending. The journey down seemed to go on forever; forward vision nil, side vision nil. Just a steep fall and her beating heart and the cry she just couldn't stop escaping.

Then the bottom. A sudden end to the chute and darkness. She found herself sailing over the edge and landing on a hard surface, jarring the bottom of her spine. Knocking the breath out of her lungs. It took a moment to recover.

Crouch held a hand out. "You okay?"

Alicia ignored the offer. "Yeah. But how am I gonna explain the bruises on my ass?"

"I'm pretty sure Drake's used to it."

"Shit, boss, what do you think we get up to?"

Jensen then flew out of the chute, landing hard. Alicia checked for broken bones and then left him lying there, wondering aloud if they might use him as a cushion for Caitlyn and Russo. But Crouch was already headed off, spotting an underground stream off to the right and following it toward a jagged row of rocks. The tunnel was now the height and width of two men. When Russo and Caitlyn arrived and dusted off they all followed Crouch.

Caitlyn showed again she was the sensible one. "Guys, how are we ever going to get back up?"

They ignored her, traveling further into the earth below Wales. Time stretched behind them without measure, a thin skein that held no sway down here. The row of jagged rocks continued for entire minutes. Sharp stones jutted up from the floor, forming trip-hazards as well as lethal weapons if anyone fell. They picked heir way carefully. Then, a wide stream barred their way, flowing crosswise to the path. Crouch bent down so that he almost touched the surface and looked both ways.

"Any traffic?" Alicia asked.

"No. Just darkness both ways. We're gonna have to jump it."

Alicia looked dubious. "Water and I don't get on. You go first."

Crouch gave her a look as if to say *of course*, then took a running jump. No way was he ever going to make it and the flow of the stream was enough to carry him away into eternal blackness, but still he tried, starting to build back up the wall of respect Alicia once had for him.

He landed short, came down hard and spluttered as he realized he'd hit a submerged ledge on the other side. Crouch crawled out of the water and waved. "You saw what to do. Let's go." He moved away at pace.

One by one they jumped and joined him. Russo allowed Jensen to make the jump alone with Alicia waiting on the other side, but the man put up no fight. Soon, they caught up to Crouch, the leader of their team taking time to examine everything as he went. They became used to walking, stumbling, traipsing on through the cavern and the odd light. It came as a surprise then when the tunnel floor abruptly ended and gave way to a terrifying vertical drop in the dark.

Crouch faltered into it, foot slipping over the edge and going straight down. Senses aware, he felt the nothingness and flung himself backwards. Still the momentum carried him forward an inch at a time, the incline sucked him down. He landed on his back, slipping over the edge.

Caitlyn grabbed the shirt over his shoulders. Alicia caught his buckle as she flung herself headlong, her own face coming close to the drop-off. Together, they hauled Crouch back to safety.

"Close," he breathed, untroubled.

Alicia didn't hear a thing, because it was she that saw it, she that found it, she that realized exactly what lay at the base of the twenty-foot drop.

"Oh, wow. You have to come and look at this."

Crouch crowded forward and then Caitlyn, Russo asking them to hurry up so he could take a turn. Alicia grinned as she leaned out over the ledge.

Below, illuminated by veins in the rock, by its own radiance and by the team's four faint flashlights, sat the biggest pile of golden treasure any of them had ever seen. Riches piled upon riches; so many gold doubloons they were uncountable, cutlasses and medallions, necklaces and bracelets and chains of brilliant gold. Gems that were the hue of emerald and ruby, and precious visions of amber and jade, all mingled within the hoard. Almost ten feet high it rose until Alicia felt she could probably jump from the ledge to the top of the golden mound and slither all the way to the ground. Crouch saw it too and the reckless intent glimmered in his eyes.

Caitlyn held out a hand. "No—"

"Fuck that." Alicia leapt first, eyes and heart and soul taken over by the wondrous sight before and below her. The leap was full of danger but she hit the top of the pile hard, the coins a solid weight against her ribs. She found purchase with her feet and slithered right down, doubloons and medallions showering around her, bouncing off her shoulders and skull and falling like rain. The bright edge of a cutlass drew blood from her arm, a sword flipped up and catapulted past her forehead. Still she fell, feet first, soles gouging a path through the chattering, gleaming pieces, displacing a mountain of wealth to each side. At last she hit the floor and rolled; rolled through jewelry and ornaments, more plunder than she had ever dreamed of.

And then came Crouch.

Soon landing at her side, eyes reflecting the glory and gleam of the fortune that they had found.

"Don't worry," Caitlyn called down. "We'll wait here so you can get out."

Alicia laughed, dug her fingers among the piles and threw a shower high up into the air. "So now is it all worth it?"

Crouch had tears in his eyes. "I wish Healey could have seen this. I would change everything if I could."

"I know." Alicia looked around and thought she spied another tunnel leading off to the right. "But we have a lot more to do yet."

"But for now," Crouch crawled around in the gold, "let's take a long moment..."

## CHAPTER FORTY FOUR

Alicia knew it was time to depart as soon as they walked away from the gold, but she stayed two more days. The Llanrumney Pub gave them lodging and help as they called in the authorities and started the long process of ensuring their find was well-guarded, kept off the front pages until required, and fought over by the right entities. That was as far as Crouch and the Gold Team went. Their passion came in finding the treasure.

On the final night they gathered at the bar, the large room warmed by a real fire, the flames crackling and sending a lustrous glow around the room. It was late evening, and the other patrons had started to drift away, but the Gold Team kept going strong, countless bottles of red wine opened before them and flowing almost as well as the laughter.

The discussed Zack Healey.

"Never as young or as naive as I wanted him to be," Alicia said. "And the poor lad always took it to heart."

"Can I tell you something?" Caitlyn leaned over. "He humored you as much as you ribbed him. Zack knows you."

"Bastard." Alicia laughed.

"Knew you," Caitlyn corrected herself. "Shit, knew you."

And there were tears, more laughter and nothing to forgive or forget. Tonight was all about Healey and the discovery he had helped make possible. Tonight was a celebration.

Tomorrow . . . they would start to mourn.

Alicia started the last bottle of wine and poured the others a glass. She held it high, the red liquid swilling close to the rim.

"To Zack. See you again, my friend."

Caitlyn wiped her eyes. "Never forget you. Never stop loving you."

"And to all those taken from us that we miss." Russo was no longer surprising them with his insight. "Friends. Fathers. I miss my dad every day. Mothers. Brothers. Sisters. Teachers," he added with a sad laugh. "Think about you every day."

What we do in life, what we are, how we treat those we love, repeats through the years in our children, our grandchildren and in our friends. Alicia thought the words, but did not say them aloud. They were too profound to be spoken aloud, too dear to her. Too emotional. She wasn't there yet.

"We'll remember you every day," she did say. "So that you never die."

The celebration for Zack Healey's life went on far longer than their rejoicing over the treasure. The memories were greater. The feelings stronger. Tonight was all about one man.

Tomorrow . . . life went on.

THE END

I hope you enjoyed the book. Alicia and the Gold Team may well appear for a fourth outing in 2017 but next up will be Matt Drake 15—the biggest and longest adventure yet for our battered, storied heroes. Due for release if all goes well in December 2016. Please follow me on social media or via the mailing list to get up to date news. Don't worry, you won't be swamped with messages. I normally only send out one informative note for each new release.
Thanks for reading!

If you don't already receive my emails and would like to sign up to my new mailing list please follow this link:
http://eepurl.com/b-xWeT

First-hand, release-related news, updates and giveaways can be found on my Facebook page—
https://www.facebook.com/davidleadbeaternovels/


And remember:
Reviews are everything to an author and essential to the future of the Matt Drake, Alicia Myles and other series. Please consider leaving even a few lines at Amazon, it will make all the difference.

## Other Books by David Leadbeater:

### The Matt Drake Series
*The Bones of Odin (Matt Drake #1)*
*The Blood King Conspiracy (Matt Drake #2)*
*The Gates of hell (Matt Drake 3)*
*The Tomb of the Gods (Matt Drake #4)*
*Brothers in Arms (Matt Drake #5)*
*The Swords of Babylon (Matt Drake #6)*
*Blood Vengeance (Matt Drake #7)*
*Last Man Standing (Matt Drake #8)*
*The Plagues of Pandora (Matt Drake #9)*
*The Lost Kingdom (Matt Drake #10)*
*The Ghost Ships of Arizona (Matt Drake #11)*
*The Last Bazaar (Matt Drake #12)*
*The Edge of Armageddon (Matt Drake #13)*
*The Treasures of Saint Germain (Matt Drake #14)*

### The Alicia Myles Series
*Aztec Gold (Alicia Myles #1)*
*Crusader's Gold (Alicia Myles #2)*

### The Torsten Dahl Thriller Series
*Stand Your Ground (Dahl Thriller #1)*

## The Disavowed Series:
*The Razor's Edge (Disavowed #1)*
*In Harm's Way (Disavowed #2)*
*Threat Level: Red (Disavowed #3)*

## The Chosen Few Series
*Chosen (The Chosen Trilogy #1)*
*Guardians (The Chosen Tribology #2)*

## Short Stories
*Walking with Ghosts (A short story)*
*A Whispering of Ghosts (A short story)*

Connect with the author on Twitter: @dleadbeater2011
Visit the author's website: **www.davidleadbeater.com**

All helpful, genuine comments are welcome. I would love to hear from you.
davidleadbeater2011@hotmail.co.uk

Printed in Great Britain
by Amazon